POSEIDON PRESS

New York

London

Toronto

Sydney

Tokyo

THE SCAPEWEED GOAT

Frank Schaefer

Poseidon Press

Simon & Schuster Building
Rockefeller Center
1230 Avenue of the Americas
New York, New York 10020

Designed by Liney Li
Manufactured in the United States of America
10 9 8 7 6 5 4 3 2 1

Library of Congress Cataloging-in-Publication Data
Schaefer, Frank, date.
  The scapeweed goat.
  I. Title.
PS3569.C343S3 1989 813'.54   88-32472
ISBN 0-671-67503-6

For Andy

Penitence must be felt as a weight.

—MONTAIGNE
  "That Our Actions Should Be Judged by Our Intentions"

THE SCAPEWEED GOAT

December 10, 1899

Never have I seen an earlier or colder winter, nor one with deeper snow. The entire valley has been blanketed since the middle of October. Many trees are entirely buried for the first time in the eight winters I have lived here. My cabin would be covered too were it not situated close to the wind scoured edge of a shallow plateau that nature has cut some three hundred feet up the steep north wall of my valley. From this vantage point I can look out over the narrow but mile long world I choose to claim as my own tho I hold neither deed nor title.

Some twenty feet to my left, or east, where the plateau is cut somewhat deeper into the mountainside, a profusion of snow has hidden Duke's shed from view, and I must keep a hole dug down to his entrance. I carry hay, a bare handful of grain, and melted snow to him twice a day. He is entirely comfortable with his shaggy winter coat and the insulation afforded him by the snow. Lonely he may be, tho I talk to him each time I visit. Harry too descends our crudely hewn snow steps, and the two of them romp as they may in the cramped space for an hour or two every day.

I am thankful for Harry. I am not lonely and need neither man nor woman for company, but a good dog is a comfort during the long winter days when even the wolves and hawks have departed for a less gelid climate where they might find food to sustain their lives.

I am not sanguine about our supplies. Marmots got into two of my grain stores and feasted prodigiously until I discovered their ravages only two days ago. There is little hay left because the snows came ere I could bring in the last cutting, so Duke is on half rations and must stay there the rest of the winter. As for Harry and me, the outlook is likewise drear. I have salt, some coffee, a sack of garlic and dried berries to keep away the scurvy, and grain enough for a poor sort of gruel for another two months, but gluttons have fouled or eaten two of my three elk meat caches. Harry cocks his head and listens intently when I tell him that he and Duke would make poor meals, but I may yet be brought to that mournful pass. Often in the past I have been forced to eat the beasts that have served me, and their meat is nourishing and life sustaining, but I do not relish the thought of eating Harry, for he has been with me ten years and I should have to boil him a long time because he has run up and down many a hill and is no doubt as tough as a boot. Were I an Esquimo, I could live on the tallow I have stored, but bear fat runs thru me faster than fire through tinder, and upsets my digestion and liver. At least I have light, and am thankful for it, for a man can sleep only so many hours in a day before his mind begins to wander in dangerous realms.

I write to fill the hours because I am tired to the death of reading these yellowing newspapers I have memorized. Newspapers are better by far than books. You can swat flies with them, carry one to help you light your fire in an emergency, and use them for a certain natural bodily function. The writing is not done by Doctors of Philosophy who pettifog a subject to death from inside a study where they never see the real world. A newspaper writer is a different sort. He spices the facts with generous helpings of bombast but few pretensions. I can chew on the meat and bones of industry, trade, and politics without choking on the guts and hair. I can gorge on insurrections and tragedies and scandals. I can sip the liqueur of learned disputations and scientific advances and the newest theories, and swallow them whole or spit them out as I will. And for dessert

I am served the light and fluffy doings of society, e.g. "Mrs. J. Shoppa was honored at a tea given by Mrs. M. Tuggle Tuesday last. Mrs. A. Monmouth poured." The news palls tho when Tuesday past was a year ago and I have memorized the words and imagined what all the actors looked like, how they were dressed, and what they gossiped about.

The truth is, I write too, after these long years, to unburden my soul. I come to this cathartic pass thru a self portrait I drew these two nights past, my first ever. You would think that a man who has been drawing pictures and painting portraits for sixty years would sometime have depicted himself. So might I have had I not a lifelong aversion to mirrors. Not that I hate them or am afraid of them, but I have ever been ill at ease with the odd looking stranger who always peered back at me out of them. Looking now at my image tacked over the fireplace, I see that I have been overly critical. A curly gray beard covers the lower half of my face. My eyes are dark, smallish, and deeply sunk into my head, but not unkindly. A brown mole out of which spring two long black hairs sits on my left cheekbone and draws attention from my nose, which is more large than noble. My pate is balding, but I have gray hair enough to cover my ears. I confess I am no beauty, but neither am I one to frighten children, which I might have known had I but thought about it, for I do not recall any child ever running from me.

And so I write as I drew, with neither viewer nor reader in mind. None the less I will wrap the paper well when I finish, for tho I seek no reader I should not be displeased if one should someday chance upon my poor literary cache. If so, he need not know my name or any other of my circumstances, for I have always been a private man. It is enough to say that the century will turn three weeks from tonight. I have seen five years more than man's allotted span but, tho I have long planned to celebrate a century of my own, must entertain the possibility that I will be denied that signal pleasure. "I fear" was on my lips, but my hand scorned the words. I do not yet fear, if ever I shall.

The tale I tell belongs to a time more than fifty years ago. Unlike Mr. S. Coleridge's Ancient Mariner, who was doomed to repeat his history to one in every three, I have held mine bottled up within me like a jinni, until the cold wind of this winter and my own mortality have rubbed me to let loose at last a short history of Home and the Noble Savages, which to my knowledge has never before been told.

And so to those events of long ago, which I can see as clearly as the paper I write on.

The year was 1845, and my bride and I, not four months wed, had moved with the spring thaw to a small valley my father and I had laid claim to during our travels in the wilderness when I was a boy. K was young and as beautiful as a wish made upon the evening star. I was not so young, as plain as a potato, and proud beyond belief that such an incomparable beauty should so much as look at, much less marry me.

K suited my taste in every way, for she was not only beautiful but strong and I wanted a woman who was no fragile flower, for pioneering was in my blood and I was determined to homestead my own place. The notion appealed to K, but her mother and father objected, for they were town people who owned a store by which they made a handsome living, and wanted their daughter to marry according to her station in life. First they forbade her to see me, but she was as resolute as she was sturdy, and opposed their wishes. Next they tried to send her to a finishing school, but she would not go. Then her father offered me money to abandon her and when I refused sent two men to whip me, but I bloodied their noses and marched them down the street thru the snow and threw them at his feet to bleed on his shoes, and told him that K and I would be married on the 1st day of the new year whether he would or no.

With that settled and the wedding behind us, they turned

their strategy to keeping us in town, for we had quickly got ourselves in a family way and they did not wish her to have the child far from help. Her father offered me a salary that would fill my pockets if I would work for him until the child was born and safely under way in his life. K was of a like mind, but I feared that one year would turn into two and two a lifetime, and I would not spend my life as a storekeeper. At last she hid away her fears and put her confidence in me, and agreed that we should set out in the springtime.

Pioneering was common in those days and most people left home with the barest necessities, so great was their desire for land of their own and a life free of the constraints of civilization. We were better provisioned, for K's father was determined that if his daughter was to go, she should be provided with such amenities as a good sized wagon drawn by a strong team could carry. For her sake I accepted the team and wagon and goods, and from my father a fine Patterson Colt .40 caliber pistol with two extra cylinders. Many began with less and acquitted themselves well, and tho K was somewhat fearful, I did not doubt that the future would treat us kindly. Pitfalls awaited us, I knew, but I was blithe and youthful, and our Bible was our ward against Satan and his evil ways and minions.

The streams were all swollen, but we forded them without loss or incident. Mottes of brush blocked our path, but my eye was quick to find the short way around and, failing that, my ax was sharp and my back strong. So it was that we reached our new home in the middle of April and found it undisturbed. A quick stream ran thru the valley's center. A small natural and well drained meadow was a blessing, for we could plant without clearing. Within the fortnight, I had plowed and set about felling trees for our cabin, and K had entrusted our seed to the nurturing earth.

I think that no two of God's children have ever been happier. We were an island of bliss. Our mare and our cow were heavy with foal and calf. Four hens and a rooster clucked and scratched, and began their task of increase. Wild game in abundance awaited my gun, and fruits and berries grew in profusion. Old Tige, a red hound my father had trained to coon, looked after us. Midway thru May, our crops were up and growing in God's sun. I had a half dozen trees down and shaped and, with the help of the gelding, laid out in the form of our house, which we sited near the center of the valley and facing south, so the winter winds would not blow thru our door, but be spent on the unbroken back wall and the thick chimney of our fireplace. There within the four low walls K and I lay at night and dreamed of the day they would rise and shelter us and our first born.

And then came our misfortune by night, and the beginning of the singular adventure that changed the path of my life as clearly as a switch changes the direction of a train. Heralded by Old Tige's growls, a strange man stumbled across our growing crops and fell insensate within the light of our fire. Had I dreamed then that he was an harbinger of death, I would have killed him on the instant or at the least let him go when, some time later, he woke with fearful eyes and a startled cry, and tried to escape us.

December 11

"For I was an hungred and ye gave me meat: I was thirsty, and ye gave me drink: I was a stranger, and ye took me in." So says the Word of God in Matthew, and so we in our innocence believed. That he was hungry was indisputable, for he was painfully emaciated and covered with cuts from thorns and bruises from where he had fallen. His clothes, which were scarce more than a breech clout and the remains of an ill made shirt, were travel worn shreds. His hair was long and unkempt, and matted with dirt and dried blood from a festering gash that ran from the center of his head to his left eyebrow.

Barely able to stumble across open ground, he was yet so strengthful when in the throes of his passion that I was forced to bind him lest he harm K when, from time to time, I sought to sleep. For three full nights and two days we were hard pressed to tend his wounds, keep him warm, and force nourishing broth between his lips and clenched teeth. On the third day he wakened when the sun was already high and asked, in the same strangely accented voice and manner of speaking that I had heard once before in an old man who had lived like a hermit for decades, if he might have aught to eat.

And so we fed him as admonished by the Lord. Weak as he was, I helped him to the water so he could bathe, and helped him don the simple trousers and shirt my wife sewed for him, for we had some little extra canvas cloth at our disposal. Presently I sat him by the fire again where he once more ate, and fell into a deep refreshing sleep.

I put my trust in Old Tige and did not tie him that night, for the few words the stranger had spoken were of gratitude, and he had no weapons.

December 16

I read once in a newspaper that gluttons, which better educated men call wolverines, are the strongest animal in the world for their size. I believe as much because the pair that has besieged me tore thru a half dozen well placed logs two nights ago to get at my last cache of elk meat. I chased them away but little good it did for they had already fouled nearly all the meat with their musk and dragged it about and slashed Harry grievously across his face when he surprised them at their mischief. I suffer for Harry, for they ripped out his eye. I have doctored him these many hours but fear he is infected despite my labors, which means if he fails to improve I must kill him before his meat is tainted beyond use. Poor Harry. Next to Old Tige, who has been dead these many years, he has been my favorite dog.

I will now describe David, as I shall call the man who stumbled into our homestead. He was perhaps my father's age, some forty or more years old. A breed, he had the hair and face of an Indian. Strangely tho, his eyes were a milky blue I had never seen in any breed I had known, much like an agate shooter I had when I was a boy, and his skin was fair but darkened by sun and weather. His teeth were firm and straight but a strangely mottled yellow and white, from a youthful fever, so K believed. He was frail but had been strong not too many days before as we could tell by his skin, which hung loose about his frame.

David slept for two days further, waking only to eat, drink, and relieve himself. From time to time he cried out in his sleep, sat up and looked wildly about him, and then reposed himself again. Altho we knew not whence he came, our sup- position was the east, for he invariably looked to that quarter. Of passing strangeness was this one habit, that he closely inspected and sniffed the food we gave him before he ate and was especially critical of the bacon K fried, for it was our only meat when I had no time to ride out to shoot a hare or squirrel or other wild game. My bride and I remarked on his peculiarity at length in private, but did not wish to be unseemly so spoke not one word to him, and trusted that he would enlighten us soon enough on his own accord.

And so the first week passed. During the second he was

much revived, and tho he spoke seldom began to help with such labors as his weakened condition permitted, viz. chopping the branches of the trees I had felled and stacking them on a sledge to carry them to the house for our winter's fuel. On the third day an exceeding strange event piqued my curiosity. I had taken my rifle with me when I went out to fell a tree, and as chance would have it spotted a squirrel that I shot for our supper. Only a few seconds later David came running to me and inquired in an agitated manner what that great noise had been.

"Why, my rifle," said I, somewhat perplexed.

"Rifle?" said he, as if he had never heard the word. "Is a rifle a gun?" he asked, staring at it in awe. "That is a gun?"

I had never met any person who asked what a rifle or gun was, and was so amazed by his ignorance that I inspected it myself to make sure it had not changed into a snake. "Why, yes."

One slow step after another, and staring at it as if he feared it would bite him, he approached me. "Wilt thou suffer me to hold it?"

"What?"

"Wilt suffer me to hold it?"

There being no danger, for I had not reloaded, I gave it to him.

The look on his face was that of a small boy given a toy he has long desired but has had little hope of receiving. His eyes wide, he held it like an ax and inspected the firing mechanism, then sniffed at the end of the barrel and peered into its darkness. "I have heard of guns," said he, "but never have I seen or heard one. Why didst thou use it?"

I pinched my leg. "To shoot a squirrel for our supper?" I asked, not altogether sure of anything.

"Where?" he asked, excited.

I pointed to a spot in a high tree some yards away. "On that branch that looks like a dog's leg?"

His eyes narrowed in suspicion. "I see no squirrel."

For answer I led the way to the base of the tree, kicked around in the leaves a moment, then held up a nice fat squirrel whose head I had shot off so he would bleed dry.

" 'Tis true, then," he exclaimed. "They do kill at a great distance!"

I confess I forgot my manners entirely and asked him how he could have got to be a grown man and never seen a gun. He answered that his people did not use them because they were tools of Civilization and in no way allowed in their land.

"But so is an ax," said I, "and you use one of them as well as any man I have known."

"Aye," he agreed. "That is true. But an ax is a primitive tool, and fit for Noble Savages. So it is that we have needles not of steel but of bone, and also pots not of iron but of clay. Our wagons are simpler than thine, scarce more than a platform with two wooden wheels, but they serve as well. Our clothes lack buttons but stay on us. We have neither forks nor coffee grinders nor waffle irons, and yet eat well enough. And we live in houses that are warm in the winter and cool in the summer, tho none of us has ever used an auger or a saw or a plane or a pulley such as thou hast."

What a Noble Savage might be was a mystery to me. K and I had agreed David was a half breed, but of what tribe we could not guess, for the Indians in those parts had been subjugated years before and their remnants driven west. I thought at first he would make further explanations, but of a sudden his face saddened and he returned my gun to me. When I pursued my inquiry more vigorously, he explained that he had fled his home and people for good reason, that he was indebted to my wife and me and should like to remain with us to learn our ways, but would leave on the instant if I persisted. With that, he set his jaw and left the choice to me, but appeared pleased when I apologized for my inquisitiveness and offered him our home and friendship as long as he should want them.

The friction between us faded, and we continued our labors in the days that followed. The wound on his scalp healed quickly after he taught K an improvement to the poultice she had made from the herbs that grew in abundance thereabouts. Soon enough he regained his strength until he could work as hard as I, and for a reward I taught him how to shoot my rifle and let him fire one cylinder full of rounds from my revolver. And tho he continued to show his gratitude for our hospitality, he said not one word more of his people or his flight.

December 20

Four days have passed since I last took pen to hand, for I have been in a foul mood since killing Harry. I do not mind killing horses, for they are generally stupid beasts, but a good dog who has been a comrade is a different tale. Many was the time Harry saved me in a scrape or comforted me when my spirits were low, and he deserved a better fate than to be made into stew. Faithful dog! He sustains me still! I threw his poor infected head to the gluttons in the hope that they will gorge on it and die.

Withal, my little cabin is a lonelier place now. Last night I filled my pipe with the herb of dreams, so called by the Indians who ruled the lower elevations of these mountains before the white man subdued them. The smoke afforded me some comfort and pleasant dreams, and tho I woke with the stiff bones of an old man, I had too another and more pleasing stiffness that belongs to a young one.

Seldom in my life have I labored harder than during that summer, and never have I more heartily welcomed hard labor.

David's strength returned rapidly, and he and I hewed and hauled and raised timbers from cock crow to after sunset, then filled our bellies and sharpened our axes and straightaway fell into a stuporous slumber. Sweating under the same sun and carrying the added burden of our unborn child, K cared for our crops, gathered and dried herbs and berries, kept our clothes in repair, and cooked prodigious amounts of food.

How I should have built a cabin alone in one summer I do not know. Together tho, David and I fairly raced thru the task. Three days a week we spent in the woods felling and trimming and shaping. One day we spent hauling, and two more fitting and setting logs in place with the help of a tripod, block and tackle, and the gelding and Old Tige, who barked encouragement. On the last day of June the walls stood a full hand higher than the top of my head, and on the 4th of July, an auspicious occasion, we set the ridge pole. By way of celebration, K unwrapped the set of china cups from her trousseau and I unlimbered one of our two jugs of whiskey. David, who had never drunk any spirits before, took to the whiskey as any red Indian will, but swore the next morning that he should never touch a drop again. Would that he had erred in his prediction!

Dare I call our lives idyllic? I think so. My body was as hard as the timbers we shaped, and as resilient. My soul was joyful and unencumbered. K glowed with health and, tho often tired, carried herself like a queen about to bear an heir to the throne. Haltingly at first, then with increasing confidence, David imitated our manners and speech. A quiet, amiable man, he was first to wake in the morning and last to sleep at night. He was ever ready with a helping hand and a smile, and had many clever tricks of carpentry that were at once instructive and beneficial, for tho I knew the woods better than most men, I knew little of construction. Thus it was that we should have had a shoddy fireplace and no mantel were it not for his handiwork, and neither shutters that fit tight nor a sturdy loft where we might secure our belongings against the elements.

Thus it was, too, that we had music from the reed pipes he made, and fresh fish from his traps, constructed of switches and sunk overnight in the deep hole near the willow brake downstream from our cabin.

Indeed, the multitude of tasks that awaited us at every hand left us neither time nor inclination to question David, and our curiosity was quite stemmed in all regards save his behavior on the Sabbath. Then, while I read Scripture aloud, he was wont to sit himself some feet apart from us and stare into the distance, and when we prayed, would bow his head respectfully and mumble amen but nothing more. Thinking that the Noble Savages he had spoken of practiced some heathenish religion, tho what form it might take we could not divine, we refrained from admonishing him, troubled tho we were for the state of his soul.

December 22

I woke this morning to find Harry's skull, which the gluttons had delivered while I slept, at my door. They had eaten it clean, but I know it was his. They must be demons, for what other kind of being can consume pustulence without ill effect? May they be damned to eternal Hell!

Tho it be the natural course of events, the weather is a pox and an abomination. It has been blowing and snowing a full white blizzard since daybreak. Now it is as dark as night tho it be but noon, as I surmise. I am trapped like an animal in a cage of its own devising, and dare not venture out farther than my porch to fetch in snow, much less seek out the gluttons. I can only hope that Duke is well, for the entrance to his poor dark cave must surely be filled in. He had some little hay left this morning, but if his water freezes will have to make do as best he can until the storm subsides and I can break my way thru to him.

I smoked another pipe of herbs last night, the first time ever I have smoked them two days in succession, and in my dreams relived the events that brought an end to the idyllic life we lived.

Our travail might have been avoided had we heeded the warnings of Old Tige, how he brings to mind the faithful Harry, but our vigilance was so much relaxed by the felicity of our valley that we did not believe anything could be amiss. The time was at the end of August when, one eventide, he commenced to act queerly, to gaze toward the hills to our east, and to smell the breeze and whine. David noted the dog's agitation immediately and displayed a nervousness I had not observed in him since his early days with us. Unconcerned myself, I urged him to dismiss his fears and assured him that Old Tige smelled nothing more than a bear or a mountain cat, for they lived thereabouts. Somewhat calmed, he never the less kept anxious watch over his shoulder all evening, and that night forsook his pallet outside our door for a spot in the deep woods, where he said the solitude better suited him.

The next morning, I well remember, we had a rain that we badly needed, for our crops had begun to parch. Declaring a day of thanksgiving, and because K was weary and troubled by the child she was carrying, we sat in front of our cabin under the small roof we had finished two days earlier and read Scripture and recreated ourselves. K busied herself carving toys out of soft wood for our child, who should have been supplied for a lifetime at birth, and I drew likenesses of K and Old Tige on a slate, for paper was dear in those days and impossible to come by in the wilderness. Birds whistled in the forest and a pair of mockingbirds that had built their nest nearby regaled us with song. Old Tige lay stretched out on his side at my feet and, his alarms of the day before forgotten, snored peacefully. The sound of the gentle rain falling was soporific, and its smell as it soaked into the dry earth was as sweet and pungent as the aroma of roasting corn and baking bread. And as I sat, my heart swelled with love for K and our child, with contentment and gratitude for the gifts God had given us, and with pride, for which I prayed I would be forgiven, for our accomplishments.

A man learns wariness in the wilderness, but learns also to distinguish between real and imagined danger. I had learned those lessons well as a child, for I had lived in the woods more than in even the rudest of shelters. So it was that I was instantly alert when Old Tige waked with a growl in his throat and his hackles rising, and so too that I relaxed when a moment later David emerged from the woods on the far side of our field. Almost comical, Old Tige looked back and forth in confusion between David and the willow brake. "You are seeing spooks, Old Tige," I laughed, scratching his ear.

Sighing an old dog's sigh, he lay his head on my knee and looked up at me, then with a brief glance at David, back at the willows.

"If he could talk," my wife said with a low chuckle, "I wonder what he would tell us."

"About rabbits and coons," said I as the sun broke thru the clouds. "Little else."

I was more concerned about David than Old Tige however, for tho he had put on a good face I could tell from his bearing that he was hiding a case of the nerves. "Have you had a good ramble, David?" I asked as he approached.

"Aye," he replied, adding the lie in his voice to that in the cast of his shoulders.

I watched him rinse his mouth and spit and then drink deeply. "Nor sign of bear nor cat?"

His eye followed Old Tige's gaze to the willow brake and he shuddered, someone walking on his grave. "Nair one," said he.

I have learned since to better regard the warnings given by dogs, and to be vigilant when men lie, but I was gay and merry then and, tho ever watchful of nature, which cares not one whit for a man's well being or life, not overly distrustful of any man I had not provoked. And so I dismissed the warnings that were given me, and my wife and I thanked God for the blessing of His rain, and passed the day in blissful ignorance of what the night would bring.

December 24

I have walked forty miles in a long day without being wearied. I have dug a year's supply of nuggets from my mine and been refreshed by my labors. I have packed an hundredweight of meat over a mountain in my seventieth year and reveled in the exercise. I have drawn pictures since I was a child, and sometimes made my living at it, but to fill three pages with words is a task for which I am ill fitted, and the labor cramps and vexes my hand and leaves my back stiff and my eyes rheumy.

Duke is well enough tho his ribs show. I have said that horses are stupid beasts and so they are, and yet a spirit resides in them, for he misses Harry and rests his forehead against my chest and nickers and would follow me when I leave him to his dark loneliness. I may yet have to sleep with him because the gluttons are a constant danger who will not forever be stayed from fresh horse meat which I must save for myself if I am to last until the thaw and not become meat for them myself, as I have seen happen in these mountains. For as a man in his travail will eat a dog or any other meat, so will a glutton eat a man, who is meat as much as an elk or a fish or a grub.

Such thoughts were foreign to my mind on our thanksgiving day. We feasted that eventide. A fat young cock and a dozen ears of fresh sweet corn roasted, some tart but tasty roots shown us by David, who knew secrets of the woods that I had never dreamed, packed in mud and baked in the coals, and a blackberry pie sweetened with honey from an open hive, hanging from an oak tree, that I had smoked and robbed by breaking off a slab of comb. Later, all sated with our stomachs full, David retired to the forest and my wife and I lazed about the fire that kept the musquitoes from us, and bantered as ever over the name we should give our child. If a girl, K cast her ballot for Sally and I for E, which was my mother's name. If a boy, I cast my ballot for J after my father and she for F after hers. Not until clouds covered the moon that was high in the sky did we give way to drowsiness and creep to our bed, where we stayed awake for a few sweet and gentle moments of pleasure before succumbing to a deep slumber.

What faint unnatural sound woke me I knew not, only that I was awake with a chill in my bones, and lay watching the dim light that distinguished the open doorway from the black night around us, and listening to the sounds of the woods. Only then, and too late, did I recall Old Tige's growls and raised hackles, for tho I could not believe our dog would let a stranger pass unchallenged, I sensed a presence in the cabin, and eyes upon me.

My wife lay asleep at my side. Save for David we had seen nor hide nor hair of any other man in that place, and believed ourselves alone. But my senses did not lie to me and, unless I was dreaming, a man was in my cabin and Old Tige lay slaughtered outside my door. So it was that, feigning some discomfort, I sighed aloud and turned to lay my hand on the hilt of the broad knife I kept holstered on the bed rail, for no wise man sleeps in the wilderness without a weapon where he might reach it quickly and wield it against whatever man or animal threatens his life and safety.

"Loose not thy blade, man," a low voice said from across the room on the instant I moved. "We intend thee no harm."

He spoke gently, as to a friend or companion, but I knew better and the blood froze in my veins.

"We seek the Wanderer who hath conspired against his own kind." The speaker paused, then continued in an accent and rhythm similar to David's. "Pray thee. Return him to us so we mought depart in peace."

My wife slept on. Prudently, for I knew not whether "we" was two or three nor where the others might be lurking, I did not pull my blade, but kept my hand close to it.

"How should I know this Wanderer you speak of?" said I in as low a voice as my interrogator's.

"We ken he be here," came the cool response. "We did see him."

I am nothing if not loyal. My father did not raise me to deliver a friend into his enemy's hands. "From the willows," said I, to buy time.

"Aye. So we ask again. Where be he?"

"I know not," said I truthfully, wondering at their great stealthiness. "Mayhaps outside the door this very moment. Why do you seek him?"

"He hath transgressed, and must be punished."

He spoke to the point, and tho I was a rustic and uneducated, I had read our Constitution and believed a man should have a fair trial as promised, especially if he was a friend who shared my board and had helped build my house. "Perhaps he does not want to be punished without a trial," said I.

"Men lie murdered, and he hath been found culpable by a trial."

"At which he was present?" asked I.

"That is of no concern to thee."

"In my ignorance, then," said I, "I deem it a matter between you and him."

26

I tried his patience, I could tell, yet he remained courteous. "Thou hast sheltered him and given him of thy repast."

"Aye, and will not give him to men who slaughter my dog."

"We will bring thee a young and handsome whelp to take the place of thy old and feeble spaniel, who failed thee."

Tho macabre, our conversation 'til then was as reasonable as any heard in the halls of Congress, but neither then nor now could I countenance sarcasm or a slur against Old Tige, who had been no more a lap spaniel than a lynx is a tabby cat.

"Damned be your whelp, if you will speak in such manner," said I, gently loosing the blanket from around my wife with one hand and grasping the hilt of my broad knife with the other. "And damned be you for a pack of murdering scoundrels!"

He was no fool that would remain in the same place whence he spoke, and would move to his left lest he was magic and could pass thru thick timbers. Like a fisherman casting his net, I hurled my blanket at the spot I supposed him to be, and followed my woolen shield with my knife before me.

As I supposed, he waited me in confidence. The blanket tho, being the same hue as the darkness, confounded him. A missile from another hand hummed like a bee past my head but I ignored it, thinking to dispatch my sarcastic interrogator first and worry about such others in due time.

I have always been nimble in a fight and without fear, which is a natural gift. Time itself slows, and tho I am little aware of thought, I am all aware of everything about me, and canny and swift and strong. Ere he knew how close I was, I had slipped around behind him and grasped him by the neck and plunged my broad knife upward thru his vitals to his heart.

"J!" my wife cried out, awakened and alarmed.

The blood gushed from him and he expired with a sigh. "We are attacked!" cried I, losing my grip on the hilt of my knife, it was so slippery.

Our battle had been eerily silent save for the soft pad of feet and that one strained sigh, so I can not blame my wife for being frightened. "Who is here, J!" she called and, as I could tell from the creak of the ropes holding our shuck mattress, sat up in our bed.

"Stay down! Stay down!"

"Oh!" cried she. "Oh! I am stung by a bee!"

"Stay down! Stay down!" cried I again, as I feared for her life.

Our cabin did seem filled with bees, but I avoided them by using my dead assailant as a shield and then, casting him aside, my blanket. Kneeling, I groped about in the darkness until I found the knife that but seconds before had been wielded against me and, slicing my little finger as I did so, grasped the blade and hurled it in the direction whence came the bees. To my relief I was rewarded with a muffled oath and a rush of footsteps out our door. Spare moments later, as I crouched in readiness, David whistled from outside and announced that all was safe.

The attack was over, and I thanked God that our lives were spared.

December 26

—————————————————————————————

Yesterday was Christmas if I reckon right, and tho I have not celebrated the birth of Christ for many years, the holiday often saddens me, and so I did not write but sat and thought upon what might have been. This is the one good reason I can imagine for ticking off the days on my calendar: that I can pity myself at the appropriate times.

When animals fight and stop, they cease altogether and go about their affairs as if they had not a moment earlier been biting and scratching and attempting to kill one another. Men are different, for they are not readily calmed once the heat of battle is upon them. I was a strapping youth. Towering well above my fellows, I stood a hand over six feet. My shoulders were wide and my arms thick, my chest bulky and my thighs like tree trunks, and I was strong from a clean life and hard labors and a willingness to trust the Lord. So too was I cheerful save when provoked, and calm in the face of such adversity as I had known. Well outfitted for a brawl as I was then and for many years thereafter, still my hand shook with apprehension when I plunged a torch into the coals of our fire and viewed the havoc wrought.

Old Tige lay at peace in the wet dirt without a mark on him save for a small rent in his side from which his life blood had flowed. Inside, I saw my wife lay in a faint from fear, and covered her with our blanket before inspecting the assailant I had dispatched. He was a man of my age and then some; his hair was straight and as long as David's had been when he came to us. His mouth agape and his bowels and water loosed, he lay where I had felled him. Tho painted in a strange pattern of heavy blotches of light and dark, he was white and not an Indian. Plucking my broad knife from his vitals, I followed a thin trail of blood across our hard packed dirt floor and out of doors, whereafter it disappeared in the wet grass. Some yards away, David stood over the corpse of another painted man he had dispatched, and I approached him with anger in my heart.

"It is good for you that my wife lives," said I, still agitated, "for were she dead I should kill you on the spot."

David hung his head in shame as befitted one who brings trouble to a benefactor. "I searched for them but found no sign," said he in a low voice.

"Yesterday morn when Tige sounded the alarm?"

"Aye. Even then. I should have warned thee they mought come. Truly, I be culpable."

"Of murder too?" asked I, recalling my assailant's usage of that word.

His head rose and his eyes flashed in the torchlight. "That be another matter," said he, and then, his brow furrowing, "Art thou wounded?"

"No," said I, having forgot my finger in my passion.

"Nor nick nor scrape nor sting of bee?" he asked, greatly disturbed. He glanced down to my feet. "Hast stepped on a barb that pierced thy foot?"

"I tell you no."

"E'en so, I pray thee inspect thyself quickly, man, for it be of great import."

Spurred by his agitation, I inspected my bare skin and especially my feet upon his insistence and found naught but the cut on my little finger, that was already red and swollen and, as I thought on it, ached with a dull throb. "Only this," said I, showing him.

"Quickly then," said he. He drew me by the arm to the block I had for chopping and pulled out my ax from the wood. "Lay it here and let me take it off, else thou perish."

"What?" asked I, withdrawing from him and placing my hand behind my back where he could not reach it. "Lose my finger for a scratch? You are mad!"

His face was pale, and he kneeled before me. "I tell thee as thou art my friend and benefactor that thy death is imminent if we rid thee not of it." Whereupon he kissed his closed fist in the circle made by his thumb and forefinger, and importuned me with a rush of words. "I beg of thee and swear upon my life. Thou kennest not what poison lies therein, and every moment be the utmost essence, for we must see directly to thy wife!"

Whether it was the warning or the dread fear in his voice or some combination of the two exacerbated by the flickering baleful light and the bizarre nature of the events just past I know not, only that there were poisons unknown to me and a finger seemed a bargain when compared to my life. "And if you miss," asked I, pretending a jollity I did not feel, "and strike my hand?"

A small smile crossed his face. "I will overlay thy hand with mine," said he, "and take the greater care."

"Quickly then," said I, deciding on the instant and laying my hand on the block. "And then lead me to the fire that we may sear it."

To this day that little finger is the only part of me I have lost, and I confess I closed my eyes before the blow fell and steeled myself against the pain. Happily tho there was but little, neither when he struck nor when he placed the stump against a live coal and the stench of burning flesh assailed my nostrils, for as he explained, the poison had dulled my nerves.

I have seen strong men faint when they lose a piece of themselves and rightly so, for such can never be replaced. I myself reeled like one drunk, and would have fallen had not David reminded me that we must see to my wife, which brought me to my senses. "But she lies naked," said I when he approached our cabin door.

"Thinkst thou that I have never beheld a woman's body before?" asked he, and then quickly added, "But soft! There be no time for disputation." Reaching inside the door, he took my boots from the peg my wife had me hang them on when I was inside, and handed them to me. "Hurry! Pull on thy boots and inspect her all over for the slightest hurt, even unto the sting of a little tiny bee!"

Too befuddled to argue, and frightened for her safety, I jammed my feet into my boots as ordered, took the torch from his hand, and rushed inside. My wife still lay in a faint. Embarrassed tho I had seen her naked often, I inspected her as ordered and found no wound, but I could not awaken her and thought I detected a fever on her brow as, unnerved and shaking all over, I related to David.

"Carry her outside, man, where there be more light, and quickly!"

She seemed to weigh but little more than a feather. Distraught, I wrapped her in the blanket and carried her out the door and lay her on David's pallet, which he had placed in the moonlight. Immediately David looked closely at each pretty hand and arm, her face and neck, and ran his fingers over all her scalp and thru her hair. "Nothing," said he, and then gently, "I must see her body all over, J, and touch her too. Not lasciviously, I swear to thee, but as a surgeon, and neither she nor any other of this world will ken what I have seen."

It was not an easy thing to watch another man inspect my wife, and harder yet to forbear from violence upon his touching her. So flushed was her face in the white moonlight tho, and so labored was her breath, that I was weak in my knees and stood by with never a word. His eye was thorough, his hands nimble, and tho I flinched when he ran his fingertips over and around her sweet breasts, I thought breath would fail me when he peered intently at a spot beneath her left one and plucked from it some small thing before covering her over again and rocking back on his heels.

"The bee that stings," said he with a sigh. Standing, he showed me but would not let me touch the burred piece of iron no bigger than a grain of corn that had been embedded in her skin, and that now lay in the palm of his hand. "The Wasp of Death."

December 27

Never since have I been so struck to the quick of my soul. That I had killed a man, my first, that my dog had been slaughtered, and that I had lost a finger were but trifles when laid beside this dire news, for such was the night and the ominous quality of David's voice that I believed him on the instant, for God only knew who his people were and what arcane arts they practiced.

I pride myself on the strength of my character, that I do not unduly anticipate the future but, having prepared myself as any prudent man would, wait the due course of events with an untroubled heart. In this matter I have fashioned my life after the animals who are wise in their own ways. But on that early morning, for light was breaking, I confess I acted the babe and sat beside my wife and held her pretty hand all hardened by her labors and stared into her face, which was beautiful beyond all others to me.

None of the events I have described would have occurred had David not found us on the night of his travail, but I know now such thoughts are senseless, and I believe K and I both should have died that day had he not been our friend and our surgeon, for I was of as little use as a tick in a dog's ear. He built a lean-to and a raised pallet so my wife should have protection from the sun and yet receive the fresh and healing breeze. He made me put on my clothes and dressed my stump with a clever poultice of herbs that drew out the infection before it started. He laid fresh poultices on my wife's chest every hour of the day and night without sleeping. He fed me warm soups and poured herbal infusions down my throat. He disposed of the corpses of Old Tige and our assailants, and cleaned within our cabin to remove the Wasps of Death that lay about the floor and in our bedding. He led me to relieve myself and, telling me to turn away my head, cleansed my wife's body which in my unnatural torpor I allowed him, for I was dulled beyond sensibility.

Two days and two nights he cared for us like children while my wife lay insensate and I sat useless by her side. Late on the morning of the third day, my wife opened her eyes and looked at me and spoke as if she had not slept one wink. "Oh J," said she, "a bee has stung me and I am burning."

Her voice was a strong potion that revived my senses. On the instant, I ascended through the fog that had cloaked me. "Yes," said I, for I did not want to trouble her with the truth. "You have been stung by a bee and must lie still." So saying, I stroked her brow with a cool cloth and called for David, who waked from a doze and came to our side.

Never has a wife been so tenderly cared for. David bade me change her poultice while he stirred some soup. After she had drunk, I bathed her all over with cool cloths to bring down her fever and fanned her with a branch of leaves until she slept again.

"Thou shouldst sleep too," said David some hours later when I drew apart to speak with him.

"I have slept two days straight," said I, "and now need answers more than sleep. Will she live?"

"I ken not," he answered truthfully, "but will give thee such answers as I have if thou wilt suffer me to dress thy hand, for I have not since early this morning, and it will fester."

And so I gave my leave and so he spoke as he worked, and tho I can still hear the stilted cadence after these many years, I find it laborious to imitate the effect, and will no longer hew to it for every word he spoke.

David told me our assailants were called Guards, who were the protectors of Home, which was the place whence he came. The poison, which was a mixture extracted from several plants, was insidious. Without certain remedies that he knew, she would surely die. With them her life depended on her constitution. Live or die, we should know after the crisis came at the end of the seventh day, and from it she would either slip into eternal slumber or wake recovered on the morn.

"And the life of our child?" asked I.

He could not say, for he could not guess how the poison would affect a fetus, nor was he a midwife.

"Then we must find one," said I, rising and ready to hitch our team to our wagon, great tho our mare was with foal.

"No," said David, restraining me by my arm. "We dare not move her, for I tell thee she shall surely perish if we do. Better," he added gently, "to yield the child to death than lose her, for she may have another."

I could find no fault with such reasoning, for the death of a child is a sore burden but a lighter one than the death of a wife.

"Then we wait," said I, determined to spend any effort to save her. "You will instruct me and I will do anything that man can do. If she live, so be it and thanks be to God. But if she die?" A murderous intent rose in my gorge and I looked to the east whence had come our assailants. "But if she die I will avenge her, for had we killed a score and another dozen in addition to the three, the price would not be paid. What say you?" said I. "Will you show me the way?"

"I cannot answer that," said David, "for we need not go to them if they come to us. Remember, J, we did slay but two."

"Hah!" said I. "I heard the last cry out and saw his blood on my floor. He was stuck with the selfsame blade that poisoned me, and he travels. Ergo, he will die."

"Aye," agreed David. "But when?"

"Why, posthaste," said I in my wisdom. "He bled profusely. The cut was deep, the poison deep within him. If I should die from a little nick so must he from a great wound, for he can neither cut off his leg and run nor excise his vitals and live."

"Fagh!" said David, spitting to one side in anger, the first I had seen in him. "Were wishes thoughts, thou wouldst be a wise man." As to a child, he held up his hand and ticked off his fingers. My blanket had two holes in it from my assailant's slim blade, which wiped off some of the poison. He was a Guard, one who becomes inured to the Wasp of Death by scratching himself and rubbing in minuscule amounts of the poison from the beginning of his training, and could survive all but a massive dose by lying down for a day or two and purging his blood. He was young and resilient, and carried remedies that would stave off the effects of the poison. And above all, he would deem his life but a trifle compared to his duty, and his determination would see him to Home. To die there quite possibly, but only after sending his fellows on the way to search us out, for they wanted David at all costs.

I did not then enjoy being made the fool. Neither do I now. But from his speech I learned anew as every young man must that a little knowledge is a dangerous possession and that wishful thoughts do not true thinking make, so held my peace. "The answer is clear then," said I, chagrined. "Who ever these Guards may be they seek you, and tho you are my friend and have saved our lives, we have saved yours too and you must go to them. For even as I would not give you over to the man I killed, so you have no right to give us, my darling K especially, over to them."

"Yes," said David, "and no. For tho I paint a dark picture, I will tell thee the other side of the coin that thou hast never seen before."

As bleak as our prospects, we were not without hope, for it was still possible that the wounded one would die before he reached Home. If he did, one of the Guards' great strengths might be turned into a weakness, for they were trained from youth to leave no sign of their passage thru the woods. Thus even were he found his fellows could not easily follow his trail to our valley, and knowing only our general direction should need an extra day or so to find us, by which time we would be gone. Also, since the poison was wont to take ominous twists and lethal turns that I would not know how to interpret or treat, he feared to leave. Unless I wished him to, he added cleverly, laying a difficult choice at my feet.

When I was a young man I was ofttimes swayed by others' arguments, for I did not always know my own mind. On that day, bereft of my old dog, with my wife at death's door, and I myself ill, I knew not how to resolve the contradictory arguments laid before me. Thoroughly confused, I sat in silence and weighed my choices, to bid him to leave or stay, in an attempt to discern which had the more merit. Finally, deciding that I was still grossly ignorant, I equivocated.

"Tell me of this Home you speak of," said I. "And of Guards and Wanderers. And murderers too," I added, seeking to know the story at greater length before I chose one side of the coin over the other.

David hesitated, and sat in silence with his eyes turned toward the east. "That will I do tho it is forbidden," said he at last, rising as he spoke and pouring a cup from the kettle that hung over our fire. "First tho, we needs must remember that thou art ill and must drink thy medicine if wouldst be strong again."

December 29

There are times when a man must be content with the knowledge at hand and set his course on the instant. There are other times when he is better served to sleep the night on the matter. One of the advantages of age and experience is that a man can more easily choose the wiser of these two paths according to the time and circumstances. I choose well now but am sure that David knew best in those long ago days, which is why he slipped into my drink the potion that dropped me into a restful slumber that prepared me for the revelations of the following days.

Sleep I did and soundly thru the twilight and the night, so I awoke refreshed in the early morning light. My wife still slept, and her fever was somewhat abated. Our mockingbird trilled merrily upon the tip of a tree. A zephyr from the south was sweetly laden with the aroma of the wild flowers which grew in profusion thereabouts. And I, a little wiser for being a day older, understood on the instant what David had done to me and did not hold a grudge, for I was so much a new man that I knew forthwith that the younger one of me the day before had been distraught beyond understanding.

I was calm that morning. I stretched and yawned and scratched myself and drank some coffee that David had brewed. I made my way to the shelter of the willows where I relieved myself of much foul material that had collected in me, and dove naked into the stream and scrubbed my body with the sand that lay on the bottom and wallowed there gazing into God's heavens as the sun turned the horizon as orange as the stirred embers of last night's fire. And when my ablutions were finished and I had eaten my fill, David bade me join him in the shade and swore me to secrecy, for there were those he loved who were in danger in the place he called Home, and he would not have them come to any harm from his own indiscretions.

I kept that oath for more than half a century, and break it now only because I need no longer hide my shame. In any case, it matters not. Home would no longer exist had I never gone there, for without a doubt it should have been discovered and destroyed either in the ill conceived and bloody War between the States or by the overbearing press of population in our country, for there is scarce a place even in these mountains where a man may be alone, much less in the east which I have read seethes with humanity, if that is what you will call it.

Even so, I am reluctant to begin. Last night in a dream I saw the head of a Guard I killed, not the first one, on the body of a glutton, and woke shaking with fear that their belief is true and that the dead return to live in the guise of animals until their sins are expiated. In days gone by I laughed that any man could contrive such a droll theory, much less believe it, but alone in this buried cabin with the wind howling and the snow eddying and the high clouds rushing across the pale sky, I am led to wonder. Is it possible that the Guards have returned to haunt me as gluttons, and steal my meat and starve me to death?

My hands shook this morning when I scraped the last of the stew I made of Harry from the pot and reckoned my stores. The tally was meager: one haunch of elk I had managed to save, one bony horse, an half an hundredweight of mixed corn and oats, and a quarter sack of flour, plus berries and garlic, salt, and a scant pound of coffee, and one tin of peaches that I have saved to celebrate the thaw when it comes. And so I faced a dilemma. Should I spend my grain keeping Duke alive, meat on the hoof? Or should I slaughter him and so destroy the only friendly living being for miles about? Dead he would give me the strength to walk out, but alive he was company, and with the great weight of eternity pressing on my soul I believed that company, even a stupid beast of a horse, was as important as sustenance.

I was in the depth of my gloom when I heard a tiny scratching in the box that holds my stores. On the instant I took up a stick and sneaked across the room and pulled away the top and saw a tiny mouse chewing at the corner of my sack of flour. Enraged, I had just raised my stick to squash him flat when he sat up on his haunches and sniffed the air and peered at me with his innocent eyes. Why my hand was stayed I cannot say, for I have killed elk and moose and horses and dogs and every kind of animal. Instead, my heart softened to the little rascal, and I reached down a finger to him which he smelled before returning to his task. "No no, little mouse," said I, catching him up in my hand where he lay quivering.

Boredom combined with apathy can unleash a great expenditure of energy, and given a reason not to take up my account, I set to work. The mouse residing for the nonce in my pocket, I cut small holes for air in a biscuit tin that I lined with a patch cut from a rabbit skin. I contrived a bowl for water out of the lid of a used peach tin, and smashed the rest flat and fixed it to the hole in the rear corner of my store box. Then I put the mouse in his new home and gave him half a dozen corn kernels and sat down to watch him.

Seen close, he was a handsome little fellow. No longer than my thumb, he weighed but a puff more than a breath of warm air. He was black all over with black beads for eyes and long whisker hairs that twitched comically. Fearless, he explored his new home before he sat down to eat one of his kernels and then store the remainder under his rabbit skin rug. His meal finished, he washed himself by licking his paws and rubbing his face with them, and then curled up in a little ball and went immediately and trustingly to sleep. For an hour I sat and watched him and at last, all smiles for the first time in weeks, named him Andrew for a brother I had these many years ago whose nose was long and pointed and whose eyes twinkled with mischief.

I do not pretend to understand the surprises that wait for a man in unlikely places, or how a great boon becomes a scourge or a scourge a boon, but only that this happens. For it came to me that the same rodents that had eaten my stores had sent me one of their kin to assuage my loneliness. I know a mouse is an unlikely companion, but I know too that he has advantages over a horse, for he eats less and may be carried about in a pocket or held in the palm of a hand. Even were the weather to break tomorrow and I should eat my peaches early, Duke would be too weak to carry me by the time the trail out of here is passable, so I saw no reason to waste another handful of grain on him. Without delay then, I closed Andrew in his tin, loaded my gun and threw my parka over my shoulders, and went out to do what had to be done.

It is no simple matter to butcher a horse, but the task is done. As much of his meat as I could I stuffed in the cubbyhole cut into the rock behind my cabin where it butts against the mountain. The rest of him lies in his dugout with the door well barricaded against the gluttons. I cut a peach tin into slivers and stuck them in the guts and threw them out all steaming on the snow in the hope that the gluttons will gorge on them and slit their innards and die, which would be another boon.

This morning I was sick at heart and faced the day with dread. I dreamed of a tub of hot water to soak my bones in. I dreamed of tea and honey or a piece of hard candy. I wished I had a newspaper that was less than six months old. I wished that outsiders had not moved into my low winter valley which I had for eight years, and failing that, that I had told them to go and piss up a long rope. Now it is night and I am again at ease. The wind is abated and I no longer fear the glutton with the face of a Guard. Andrew and I are well fed and he sits on my table and watches me while I write. I will tuck him in his box when I finish and go off to bed myself, and in the morning begin to recount David's tale and the horrors of Home.

January 1, 1900

New Year's Day, as I reckon it. As good a day as any to begin, in my own words tho with what I hope is some little flavor of his, David's story of the Noble Savages and their Great Experiment that he feared was as doomed as an Outsider stung by the Wasp of Death and allowed to continue on his way untreated.

The Noble Savages lived in a valley much like my wife's and mine tho vastly larger in every aspect. This valley, Home as it was called, lay three days from us at a fresh pace to the east and somewhat south, which was off the beaten path in those days. No Outsider had entered there and left again to report his discovery for as many years as the oldest among them could remember, for Civilization was feared above all things natural or made by man.

The Noble Savages were led to Home by a great man named Jack Cunningham. David's great-grandfather Ralph, who had been the foremost herbalist and the oldest living man among the Noble Savages, died at an advanced age some thirty-five harvests earlier, when David was a lad of ten, and remembered Jack well and spoke of him often to David. When he spoke, his eyes glowed as he recalled the early days and their travails and labors, and the dream they had shared.

Jack Cunningham was an Englishman before his band of travelers forsook Civilization and journeyed to Home. He was a large and hairy man but clean shaven except for an unruly mustache that hung below his chin. He was titled and a man of letters, an adventurer and a trader, and above all else a seeker after truth, wherever it might be found. He had journeyed the world over even to India and China, whose noble peoples in ancient days had lived according to the precepts of great truths, he believed, but had been trammeled into the dirt by Civilization and Government, which was Civilization's hand maiden. On his return to England he had stopped in a city he called France, as David had it, where he obtained a proclamation made by a learned man, and it was as if a torch had flamed in his head. Rich in the way Civilization measures wealth, he envisioned an historic combination of what he had learned in the Far East and what the learned man in France had said, and set about gathering followers to accompany him on a journey that would take them far beyond England and Civilization to the banks of the great River of Truth itself.

Their way was not easy, for as oftentimes is the case dreamers undertake tasks that demand prodigious efforts if they wish to survive the rigors that challenge them. After two years of planning and gathering people and supplies, they set out on their odyssey in the early spring of what I reckon was 1757 with three ships to sail the wide Atlantic. On these three ships were eighty men of whom fifty had wives, eighteen children of varying ages, plus provisions for one year of life. The journey was marred by storms and illness and dissension among the Dreamers, as they called themselves, but Jack Cunningham held them together the way glue holds a chair in one piece, and all survived to help build carts, which they loaded and hitched to oxen they bought, and set out to the west.

America in those days was vaster for all its emptiness of people. The city on the coast quickly gave way to countryside and towns and villages, then hamlets and scattered settlements and the crude homes of individual settlers, and finally the great wilderness itself, which stretched beyond the imagination. Travel was difficult, the more so because no known white man had ever stepped foot on those many hills and mountains they climbed and descended, nor wet himself in the numerous streams and rivers they forded. The woods were thick and ways had to be found thru them without cutting trees, for Jack

did not wish to leave a blazed trail for others to follow. The
musquitoes were a menace and so were all manner of flies and
gnats and other insects. Tho Jack bent his powers to make
friends of them, wild savages attacked the travelers and killed
four of their number and carried off three of their wives.

Not one among them knew where they were going or how
long they should travel or when they should stop but Jack, nor
did he either as he admitted to Ralph a score of years later,
save that he believed he should know the place when he saw
it, and without his conviction and inspiration many would have
repudiated their oaths and returned to Civilization, counting
its evils blessings when compared with the hardships of the
wilderness.

David's eyes glowed as he described how the Dreamers
crested a hill some fifty or sixty days after their landfall in the
New World and found themselves on a sheer escarpment over-
looking the valley where he was born so many years later, for
that spot had become sacred to the Noble Savages and he had
stood there often. Below them, sparkling like a jewel in the
slanting afternoon sun, a lake beckoned. To the south and
behind them to the east the valley ended in high hills. To the
north it stretched as far as the eye could see and faded into a
blue-green haze. Before nightfall they had descended to the
floor and camped on the shore of the lake, and Jack withdrew
from the rest to stand alone and pray, and then returned to
announce that they had found their Home, and took up an ax
and broke the wheel of a cart to signify that they would journey
no farther but put down their roots and make their Brave New
World, as he called it, on that spot.

And so they did, and so too by the time the first snow fell
some few months later had they made great progress, for Jack
had chosen his companions well, and each of them tho humble
was resourceful. Carpenters and other craftsmen felled trees
for cottages. Farmers cleared land for fields. Fishermen salted
and dried fish they caught from the lake. The women gathered

and dried berries and fruits and nuts and edible roots for the winter so they might save their grains for planting in the springtime. Hunters, one of them a famous poacher they had got from a prison, learned the ways of the wild animals and where they might be found and brought down. A surveyor and two others mapped the valley and, of importance to all, laid out a township which they called New Rousseau around a central square, where a meeting hall was built on their days of rest.

Uppermost in the mind of Jack Cunningham was that their colony, or Utopia, for he called it various names according to his mood, learn from the wild savages thereabouts and combine with them in order to live a more simple life and so avoid the complications and hazards of Civilization. This thru his prowess with languages and his uncommon bravery and commanding presence he was able to accomplish, and so it was that the first winter being bitter cold and the wild savages hard pressed by starvation, he bargained with them and traded blankets and knives and sundry other items for wives, of which Ralph got one, who bore him three daughters and a son who was David's grandfather.

The first three years were filled with happy conclusions to Jack's every promise and prediction. More children were born and some few wild savages joined them so their number increased to well over two hundred. Every one of them was snugly housed, warmly clothed, and well fed. They knew where to find and how to purify salt. From a natural infatuation with the healing arts, Ralph had learned the primitive pharmacopoeia of the Indians and how to make infusions and poultices for every ailment and wound. One and all, they set their oxen to the plow and, no matter what its previous occupation, each family learned to sustain itself by its own labor. Nuts, berries, fruits, and tubers became their staples in addition to fish and game and the corn and wheat they had brought with them. As quickly as they learned and mastered one simple way, they discarded the version of it they had known in Civilization. They consumed the last of their tea and rejoiced, for infusions of bark and wildflowers were tastier and more healthful. Their clothes tore and rotted away and they cared not, for breech clouts and their own skin sufficed in summer heat and the skins and furs of animals in winter cold. They learned to make bows and arrows and slings and spears. They became tanned and their skin glowed with health. Their young men ran races and competed in wrestling and hurling objects and all manner of physical prowess. And they laughed and were happy and sang songs of thanksgiving, for tho hopeful, many had been filled with trepidation at leaving the old world they knew for the new world they called Home.

January 3

It was impossible even in those days and in that place to remain isolated from the rest of the world, for tho the number of settlers in America was small, among them were many brave and hardy souls who like Jack and the Dreamers had little use for Civilization else they had not fled it. Home being so far to the west beyond where any other white man had ventured at that latitude and the way fraught with wild savages and other perils, the Noble Savages were given some time to become established. Thus isolated from the ills of the world at large, they lived in harmony with nature, and the wild savages looked on them with awe and traded with them and sometimes lived among them and learned to trust them, for Jack had kept his word that the Noble Savages would not venture from the confines of Home save to gaze on it from

Discovery Promontory, which they named the escarpment whence they had first spied their valley. And then one day came unbidden a man and his wife and three children in a cart drawn by mules, and with them a commodity that was to change the face and character of Home forever.

Because Isaiah Thomas and his wife and children were the first white Outsiders to enter New Rousseau, the Noble Savages sequestered them apart from the general population while they debated at length over their fate. Some wished to kill them immediately, others were willing to let them live if they eschewed the tools and customs of Civilization and became Noble Savages. Some were less forthright and wished to send them into the wilderness beyond Home where they would perish of animals or wild savages or starvation, for the Dreamers themselves had survived only by virtue of their numbers and cooperation. In the end, the women would not see the wife and children driven out without good cause, so Isaiah and his wife, for women at that time were deemed the equals of men and expected to speak for themselves, were questioned by the assembled Noble Savages about their history and motives. Ralph privately inspected each of the five for disease, and tho the eldest child had been infected with a cold and rash two weeks earlier, all were healthy. When the inquisition ended, the assembled Noble Savages decreed that the newcomers could either join their colony or move west, but in no case could they try to return to Civilization and survive. Their decision, which understandably was to stay, was one the Noble Savages later regretted.

Death was little known in Home and New Rousseau. One man had died of a tree falling on him, another of drowning. Two women had passed in childbirth and three babes lay in graves. Of disease or the pox tho there had been none, and the Noble Savages were robust and healthy until a week after the newcomers descended into their valley.

The youngest Thomas child was the first to sicken. The

women of the Noble Savages, who supposed the babe had taken a colic from its new diet and the lingering effects of Civilization, gathered about her mother to offer sympathy and aid, for Thomas's wife was a girl quick to smile and was generous with her stories about Civilization which, tho all professed to abhor them, fascinated especially the women who were naturally curious. Two days later, only then hearing about the child's illness, Ralph took one short look at her and recognized the symptoms of the smallpox, and tho he sent Isaiah Thomas and his family far apart from the general population, he was too late. The first Noble Savage baby was stricken a week later, and the next day a wild savage, and soon after dozens more.

I have seen smallpox and had it myself, so I know of what David spoke. In mild cases, he said, the disease began and ended with fever and a rash, and with vomiting, diarrhea, and prostration. In more severe cases the rash that started on the face and forearms spread rapidly to the upper arms and body. By the third day the lower extremities were covered, after which rose blisters that were inclined to fill with pus. Other, more terrifying, symptoms followed. Some victims bled from the mouth. In some there was a devilish itching, and the face swelled so the eyelids closed. Some contracted boils and abscesses, and others erysipelas. Only the adult Noble Savages were spared, for they had all been stricken before in England, and survived.

A terrible panic gripped red man and white alike as the disease raced thru Home and its environs. Ralph and the wild savages' shamans exhausted their pharmacopoeia but could not stay the epidemic. Within two weeks virtually every baby was ill, and the green grass in the Field of the Returned, as they called their cemetery, was marked with a pox of its own, which was the heaped brown earth of new graves. The scourge was even more devastating among the wild savages because the adults were also susceptible. With dozens of them stricken, their fellows fled to avoid the Death of the Many Agonies but succeeded only in carrying it to the surrounding population in a great spreading wave that left whole villages and encampments decimated. Those who survived were perplexed, confused, frightened, and enraged, for the white men they had taken to their bosoms had repaid them with death.

Jack Cunningham was helpless in the face of the relentless disease that took one of every two of those it struck. Helpless too against the grumbles, rising anger, and increasingly warlike threats of the wild savages who survived. He swore to them that the Noble Savages had not plotted to infect their benefactors so they might steal their land, but they did not believe him. He explained that he and the other white men and women did not contract the disease because they had survived it as children, and that once contracted it could never more harm any man. By way of answer the wild savages pointed to their dead and dying and demanded that he remove the scourge before any more of them should pass on. Greatly chagrined, Jack reiterated his love for his red brothers but swore upon his life that neither he nor any other man could stem the tide of death before it ran its course. The wild savages responded with an ultimatum that either Jack stop the disease forthwith and give food to any red man or woman or child who asked for it during the coming winter, or every white man and woman and child in the valley would die a horrible and lingering death.

Jack Cunningham was no man to fear threats, because he had been threatened before and lived to tell the tale. Neither was he a fool. Mistaken tho the wild savages were, and their population halved, they were invincible, for their number far exceeded that of the adult Noble Savages, who could no more defend Home than a handful of bees can a hive. Not one would survive a pitched battle, and Jack did not intend to have spent so much money, studied so diligently, traveled so far, and worked so hard to see his dream die on account of the smallpox or any other disease.

The summer had been long and hot and there was no time to lose, for the fields were ripe and they should starve in the winter if the crops were not harvested and stored. The Noble Savages were already exhausted from the terrible ordeal of burying so many of their children, and fear of the wild savages whose camps surrounded New Rousseau filled their eyes. And so it was that Ralph was called to Jack's cabin that night and found him pale and trembling.

"Thou must prepare a potion for me," said Jack. "I am weak all over and at my wit's end. Give me some little soporific so I may sleep the night and think the more clearly on the morrow. And do not leave my side, for I fear some wild savages will murder me as I sleep and reduce New Rousseau and its every inhabitant to ashes ere sets the harvest moon."

Ralph had such an herb and administered it to Jack, who soon slept like a babe, but in the middle of the night he waked in a great ecstasy for he had dreamed a wondrous dream that he said was the answer to their prayers, tho he did not have the complete answer. "For that, thou must be my adjutant and helpfellow, for I trust thee and the plot be but an empty scheme without thy skill in herbs. When thinkst thou that the pestilence will run its course?"

"Why soon," replied Ralph. "There be few yet who are not exposed to it."

"Aye, tho our red brothers believe me not. Hast heard of the Scapegoat of the Jews?"

"That they drove out of Jerusalem to Hades with all their sins? Aye."

"Then what sayest thou we give them such a goat, for I have read of it in books and seen the identical trick devised by other races in the Far East."

"A fine plan," said Ralph, "save we have no goats."

"That I ken full well, and so propose a man." Here he paused and fixed Ralph with a straight stare, according to David's recollection of his great-grandfather's tale. "The selfsame Isaiah

Thomas who carried this pestilence to our midst, for I am convinced our red brothers will be assuaged in no other way."

So the plan was not Ralph's, David reiterated, tho he sat with Jack Cunningham the rest of the night and between them they schemed how the plan should work, and this was it, what no other Noble Savage knew, for they did not keep their history in books and Ralph had told only David.

That morning the Noble Savages would be assembled and told that Jack had seen in a dream that one of them had brought the pestilence among them, and that they would all be given a potion that thru its mystical qualities would determine who was culpable. Into that portion given to Isaiah Thomas and his wife would be introduced some milk of the 'scapeweed, so named because it inured its taker to pain and induced a drunken euphoria. At the same time Jack would say to the wild and Noble Savages alike that he would drive the pestilence into the culpable one, who would expiate his sin by taking the pox from them and carrying it out of the world of the living, that the innocent might be freed of it. That night, with the two victims under the influence of the 'scapeweed, Ralph would secretly paint them with dots so they might be discovered the next day and moved to the meeting hall where all might see them, and on the night of the harvest moon, which was holy to the wild savages, be despatched and the next day buried in some special place that would become revered.

The plot worked. Ralph ministered the 'scapeweed to Isaiah and his wife and that night painted them all over with white and black and red dots. Discovered in the morning by their neighbors, they were taken to the meeting hall and their one child who had survived was given to a woman who had lost her own. The news spread quickly. By noon every Noble Savage in the valley and a dozen wild savages had filed past the meeting hall, that they might see the culpable ones. An hundred wild savages arrived the next day, a thousand more in the week that followed. Ever vigilant, Ralph put 'scapeweed in the water Isaiah and his wife drank so they should remain dulled to their predicament, and on the appointed day administered an herb that loosed them peacefully from their lives. The next morning Jack conducted a hastily devised ceremony in which he lavished praise on the scapegoats for their sacrifice, then led a procession to the Field of the Returned, where they were given a spot away from the other graves.

The pestilence ran its course without help of man, but wild and Noble Savages alike, all equally superstitious and gullible, were quick to believe because they wished to believe. And so were born the rituals of the Assumption of Culpability and the Gesture of Propitiation thru the Scapeweed Goat, which was the salvation of Home and the Noble Savages in that time, but not so much as an hundred years later a pestilence in its own right, and their greatest scourge and debilitation.

January 6

Unlike the gluttons who are determined to bedevil me forever, the pestilence departed and the wild savages were assuaged and pacified. The harvest was bountiful, and there was ample food for the Noble Savages to share with their wilder brothers. In the spring however, when the fields had been planted and the first sprouts showed their faint greenery, a delegation of wild savages visited Jack to sit and smoke and parley with him. They were concerned, he learned after a long afternoon of expostulation and mutual compliments, about a resurgence of the plague and wanted to know how he planned to appease the Great Spirit and so avert another catastrophe. Taken by surprise, for he had thought the matter ended, Jack employed the wild savages' own methods of procrastination and at last declared for lack of any better plan that since the Great Spirit appeared pleased by the sacrifice given Him the year before, He would no doubt be pleased again should the need arise.

The wild savages became more nervous as the summer progressed, and Jack and Ralph discussed their obsession at length. When, as it happened, a young Noble Savage was struck by a wasting disease that Ralph was unable to cure, the wild savages began leaving gifts of food and trinkets and weapons outside the young man's cabin. Soon the simpler of the Noble Savages were following the wild savages' example, and by the middle of the summer the confused and frightened man and his wife were looked upon in awe by everyone and given anything they wanted as they moved about the village. When it became evident to Jack and Ralph that red man and white alike expected the couple to be sacrificed, they were powerless to resist. A week before the harvest moon, the young man and his wife were fed the 'scapeweed, taken to the meeting hall, painted all over with dots, and poisoned to death on the appointed night. They were paid every honor and laid to rest the next day alongside Isaiah Thomas and his wife, for the people ascribed the bounty of the harvest to their sacrifice.

Jack and Ralph thought their problems were over but they were wrong, for that winter there arose a new threat to their hard won peace, which was religious fervor. All men eventually question their place in the universe and seek answers to the unknowable. In this quest two Noble Savages emerged as leaders. One was a man who preached what Ralph told David was Christianity, which he called one of the worst religions ever and blamed in part for the debasement of Civilization. The other was a woman who talked with the dead and caused their voices to emerge from the mouths of animals. By spring and the time for planting, the Noble Savages were divided in two hostile camps and verged on civil war. Jack was no more willing

to allow the destruction of his dream by religious warfare than
by the smallpox. That summer, with Ralph's complicity, the
two leaders were stricken with a strange disease, died in the
light of the harvest moon, and were disposed of in the same
manner as Isaiah Thomas and his wife.

Tho Jack had never taken a wife, neither had he ever forgone
the pleasures of women, for he was a comely and charismatic
man who attracted many of the fairer sex. But that winter he
became lackadaisical and lay with women only when one came
unbidden to him, for he had become obsessed with a contra-
diction and conundrum, which was this. He had fled Civilization in part because he hoped to escape the constrictions and
connivances and evils of religion, and yet he was forced to
conclude that there was no escape from such a social ill because
the people would have one come what may. To that end he
and Ralph, who had become indispensable to him, set about
contriving a religion that would serve the Noble Savages and
bind them together without grinding them down or enslaving
them. This they felt certain they could do because there were
no books or teachers to perpetuate the influence of Christianity,
which was perceived as a symbol of Civilization, and because
the Noble Savages were as easily led as the common herd in
any other society. Both understood that the religion they devised would be bogus, but both too had been made cynical by
the ease with which the people were manipulated, and supposed that one religion was as reasonable as another and in
any case necessary to keep Home intact.

They began with a fortuitous discovery of a phenomenon
Ralph had observed the first time while sporting with a
woman. He had taken her some distance out of town one
summer night in order to be well away from his wife, and they
lay on a low hill under the rock wall that formed Discovery
Promontory. As it happened, the moon was full that night,
and when it had risen directly above Discovery Promontory,
slight imperfections in the rock cast shadows not unlike those

on the moon itself and formed, to Ralph's imaginative mind, the apparent shape of an immense and brooding face. Ralph pointed out the face to the woman, who couldn't see it, and because other matters were more interesting at the moment, promptly forgot it.

But it was to return full blown when Jack and he later conglomerated all the gods they had ever heard of and fabricated a new one they called the Universal Infinitude. Fleshed out, the Universal Infinitude was the sum total of the universe and the knowledge therein. He had revealed to Jack, because Jack was the Noble Savages' leader, that His earthly residence was the rock wall that rose five hundred feet to form Discovery Promontory, in which His face could be seen by the faithful. Because Civilization had turned to false gods, He had caused the civilized nations to forget Him and had newly chosen the Noble Savages as His own people. Should they betray Him, He would abandon them also. But should they cleave to Him, they would spread His name thru the world when the time would be right.

The Universal Infinitude was a jealous god, so you can imagine where that came from, and decreed that the Noble Savages worship Him with certain rituals, among which were the Assumption of Culpability and the Gesture of Propitiation. He furthermore decreed that Jack establish an hierarchy of priests and soldiers to minister to and guard the common people. Jack then glued the whole together with the vision of His Face, which everyone quickly learned to recognize, and a hodge podge of other beliefs that strain the imagination. Real or bogus, Jack and Ralph's handiwork was accepted as gospel by the time Jack died some fifteen years later, and thereafter the more so because of the frequent appearance on Discovery Promontory of a great white stag in which it was supposed Jack's spirit resided.

David was murky on the evolution of the Truth, as their religion was called, but by the time he was a boy it ruled the lives of the Noble Savages, whose numbers had grown remarkably. Two new villages graced the valley, one to the north and one to the south of New Rousseau. The hierarchy had grown too, as hierarchies will, and its members had become entrenched and more noble than the common Noble Savages.

At the lowest level were the Guards. Twenty of the strongest, swiftest, and most daring of the young men were chosen every year after a grueling month long competition that began on the winter solstice. Their apprenticeships lasted three years and ended with an exhausting trial of strength, endurance, and presence of mind that weeded out all but five of the survivors and returned the others to their villages where they became minor functionaries who oversaw those who labored in the fields. Some few of the older Guards whose loyalty was beyond question were the only Noble Savages ever permitted to leave Home. Called Traders, they conducted the meager commerce between Home and Civilization, which was principally the exchange of brightly colored woolen blankets for ax heads and other necessary metal implements. The vast majority, and all of the younger ones, patrolled the surrounding wilderness to protect Home against intrusions from Civilization and to return to a certain death those few malcontents called Wanderers, who attempted to leave.

At the next level were the Adepts, as the priests were called, who by this time were all men, for women priests by their sensibilities had proven a distraction, and men were more easily molded into a body of like minds. The Adepts were Home's spiritual and temporal masters, and held their titles for life save one was declared unfit by his fellows and degraded to a common position. Five eminent Adepts, one from each village, one from those who ministered to the wide areas of the valley outside the authority of any village, and one from those who ministered to the Guards, joined in the Conclave of Adepts to choose a Preeminent One, who ruled for his lifetime. Any fourteen year old boy who wished to become an Adept announced his intent at the celebration of the New Year. Each was rigorously examined by the Conclave of Adepts, who bestowed the title of Acolyte on a fortunate ten. These ten were apprenticed until the celebration of the New Year seven years later when the best suited three received the Adept's Mantle of Feathers, which was sewn from the hides of red and blue birds.

The glue that held this system together, for that was my metaphor, came from every corner of the earth. I was ignorant of many of these customs and beliefs, as David related them to me, for I had not studied overly much on religion as a young man. My mother and father taught me to read by the Bible. I was made to understand that its every word was inspired by God, that its interpretation was inviolate, and that the Romans and Quakers and such others as called themselves Christians were in grievous error and no more Christians than the red Indians, who were heathens. So it was that I listened to David in awe and some trepidation, for I did not wish to be tainted.

I will save David's description of the transformation of the rituals of the Assumption of Culpability and the Gesture of Propitiation for another day, for they deserve a time of their own and Andrew is clamoring for my attention by staring at me and twitching his whiskers. Enough for now to inscribe a few of the Noble Savages' beliefs and whence they came.

From the Christians, Jews, Muslims, and many others, the precept that the male was the dominant force, and that the female was his consort and handmaiden and existed by his sufferance, which stripped women of their status as equals. From the Jews and divers other tribes who had invented the selfsame practice, the scapegoat. From the Muslims, a proscription against alcohol and other intoxicants, which no man could make or sell or imbibe. From the Romans, the Conclave of Adepts and the Preeminent One. From the wild savages, a reverence for nature in its every aspect be it plant or animal or mineral. Most remarkable, to my mind, from some Eastern religion, the idea that a man might die and enter the body of an animal or other lower being, which appears impossible.

I have learned over the years tho that men hold many strange beliefs, and have come to the point where I wonder who dares with certainty say them nay. One who was so inclined could argue that if Jack Cunningham and Ralph were secretly influenced by the Universal Infinitude, it must follow that their improvisations were not improvisations but rather revealed truth. Who knows, when all is said and done, what truth may be? It is far fetched but possible, for example, that Andrew's twitching whiskers are telling me the exploits of a man in mouse's language, and that the gluttons are rapacious incarnations of some evil men that I have known, for they would not otherwise have killed my dog and spoiled and stolen my meat.

But then I wonder further. If David is right and God is not an individual but the sum total of existence, then who assigns the soul in a man to a shark or a songbird, or conversely the soul in a polecat or a stinging scorpion to a man? That was one question he could not answer, for he had never thought of it himself nor had any of his fellows who he could remember. Nor could he tell me whence came the multitude of human souls that now populate the earth, for I have read that seventy-five millions now live in these United States and that a file of Chinamen might pass two abreast in front of a man for a thousand years without an end. This is a strange fact, for I have seen no diminution of animals lest it be in buffaloes and passenger pigeons, which in that case were a great reservoir for souls, for they are nearly all gone. And when I think on that, it is possible, for the vast majority of mankind has no more wit or intelligence than a passenger pigeon or a buffalo, which were the dumbest beasts that ever flew over or walked upon the face of the earth.

January 7

There have been many times in years gone by when I have thought about David and the troubles he brought me, and my gorge would rise and I would want to spit, and felt my sputum would be as evil smelling as a camel's. I have seen camels in West Texas where the army took them and then let them go to fend for themselves against the wolves and coyotes and big cats that descended from the Davis Mountains and found them easy prey. That is the U.S. or any other army I have ever read about all over again. I would not be surprised one whit if it were demonstrated that the soul of every general that ever walked came fresh from a buffalo or horse or other dull, stupid beast, for they are ever obtuse and limited in vision, and raising cockalorum schemes that harm innocent men and animals.

David was not a general, but he was a priest, and you can toss a coin to see which is worse. Many are the generals who are as much slaves to dogma as priests may be, and many are the priests who view themselves as generals in the great battle against evil and treat the common man as cannon fodder. Not all priests, I admit, for there be some among every denomination I have heard of who were devout, generous, honest, and wise men. Whence I conclude, by the by, that the brand of a man's religion has naught to do with the state of his soul or the manner in which he conducts his life. If he will be good, he will be good, if evil, evil, as history instructs with a plethora of examples.

At whatever spot David fell on the line between the poles of chicanery and charity, such thoughts were far from my mind in those days when my wife lay so ill and he talked about the Noble Savages, as much to occupy my mind with other matters else I should have drove myself mad with worry. On the day I ascended from my torpor, K rested well, waked from time to time to drink some broth and say a word or two of little consequence, and slipped back into sleep. That night she dreamed nightmares, as I supposed, for she cried out in her sleep and thrashed about so violently that David gave her a potion to calm her. On the next morning she took a high fever and suffered convulsions that shook her poor frame, and we labored all day long at her side cooling her with wet cloths. When at last her fever broke without a sweat, David studied her closely for many minutes by the light of a torch while she slept, and announced that it would drain her system to the point of death, but he must purge her on the morrow or she should certainly die.

I had given up all thought of asking him to leave, for my wife's life was more important to me by far than the distant threat mounted by the Guards. As a man will grab at the smallest straw to stay afloat when he is drowning, I had convinced myself that the one I had struck was dead and could send no others to complete his murderous intentions, or so delayed that my wife should be recovered and the three of us well distanced from that dangerous spot before his fellows should appear. Even so, I slept poorly that night during David's watch, and worse after I woke and saw him sitting on his heels some distance apart from our fire and gazing steadily to the east.

Rarely in all my years have I spent a more trying day than the one that followed. David had warned me that the purgative was strong and its effects violent, but I had put myself so much in his hands that I did not question its necessity and in any case supposed no purgative could be worse than those that country folk take from time to time to rid themselves of worms. Only at daybreak did I fall into a deep sleep, and when

I woke from it David had already administered the medicine
to my wife, whose color was good and whose mien was cheerful. An hour later she was the very picture of abject misery.
She vomited until her stomach was emptied, and brought up
green bile. Her bowels ran like water, dark and foul as mine
had the morning David began his tale of the Noble Savages.
David would not let her walk, but in no case could she have
for she was cramped and weak and dizzy, so all her excretions
had to be passed into a bucket, which was a trial.

Her ordeal lasted three hours. The tarpaulin we had hung
gave her scant privacy, for sound and smell were ample proof
of what transpired. She had never since we were married been
modest with me, but was embarrassed by her helplessness and
by my having to cleanse her like a babe. Soon enough tho, she
was too debilitated to protest or express her shame, even when
between bouts David stepped in to inspect her and stroke her
brow like a puppy's and tell her that it would be over soon and
that she was a heroine and doing marvelously well.

If ever a cure came close to killing, that was the one. K lay
limp and exhausted, drained almost of life, and I was in little
better condition for my emotions. Yet still there was work for
me to do, for the day had turned out hot and she did not want
the blanket on her, nor David to see her naked. Accordingly
David continued his tale while he prepared both hot and cooling beverages that I carried to her and made her drink, for it
was of exceeding importance that she replace the fluids she
had lost if she were to recover. Only when she passed her
water for the first time, which was near sundown, did David
declare an end to the regimen of fluids and give her a draught
that dropped her into a deep slumber.

As for me, I was at once numbed by her ordeal and grateful
that she had lived thru it, for I had had my doubts. Grateful
too that David continued his tale with no prompting, for I
could not have borne silence at that point. Even when he came
to an end for the day, I was too exhausted to sleep and was

kept awake by my nerves, so took the first watch. And after setting a smudge pot to keep away the musquitoes and covering my wife with a light blanket, for it had cooled as the sun set and David did not want her to take a chill, I sat apart from the fire for a moment of solitude.

Five and a half days had passed since the Wasp of Death had stung my wife. A day and a half remained until she should reach her crisis. David had promised nothing, but had seemed more sanguine about her prospects after the purgative had done its work, and she had regained her color and bodily functions. As for the purgative's effect on the child, I had forgotten to ask David, but supposed it was still alive because K had shown no sign of expelling it. In truth I was too tired to worry overly much about a creature I had never seen, even if it was my own son or daughter. Vastly more important was K. If she lived, as I had convinced myself she should, we would quit that place forevermore, and I would be grateful and give all thanks to God. And if she died? As had David the night before, I sat on my heels and set my gaze to the east whence they would come if they came. And if not, where lay the path I would take, and the retribution I would exact.

January 10

A man's mind may be likened to a great plain over which the waters and winds of time have swept and worn away much of the land, but left hummocks and pillars and hills of denser stuff, more durable events that persist as memory. In like manner, the events of that week of my life stand out like a great mesa that rises abruptly from the sandy floor of a desert, and all the rocks and crevices are words and sights as easily discerned now as they were when they were said or seen.

I can close my eyes and see my wife's face as she slept and when she was in pain. I can see her eyes looking into mine and read their silent pleas. I can see her hair spread on the pillow I made for her from an empty flour sack filled with the tips of fragrant pine boughs, which I can smell. I can hear David's voice, low and soft and strangely accented, and recall each word he said. But I had forgotten until this morning a way of killing gluttons that I heard only last summer when I went to Portland for my winter's supply of foodstuffs and drawing paper and newspapers. The method is used by Esquimos for killing polar bears, and was told me in a saloon where I went to drink some whiskey and buy a jug or two to bring home with me. I hope it will work better than the peach tin slivers, which they discovered and spit out on the snow.

I have for years scratched scenes on bones the way sailors do to while away the time, and had set aside some of Duke's to dry and scrape and prepare for some pictures I had in mind. When I remembered the Esquimo story this morning, I took a leg bone down after Andrew and I had broken our fast, tho he no doubt had nibbled away during the night at the grain he has stored. Immediately I carved a half dozen long slivers out of the bone and set them to soak in warm water. Next I broke thru the logs that barricade the door to Duke's shed and brought back a haunch, from which I hacked off a like number of chunks of a size a glutton might eat whole, and set them before the fire to thaw. When the bone slivers were soft, I cut slits in the meat, coiled the slivers tightly and shoved them inside, then bound each bait with a leather thong. That done, I replaced them in the cubbyhole at the rear of my cabin. When they are frozen, I will remove the thongs and set out the pieces where the gluttons may find them and gobble them up. When the meat thaws inside them, the bone slivers will uncoil and pierce their innards which will cause them to sicken and die, and I will have the last laugh.

Meat freezes as slowly as a watched pot boils, and I am writing to pass the time, for Andrew is in a sour mood and curled in a little ball in the corner of his biscuit tin where he sleeps.

I tried to share the valley with the gluttons for they are living creatures and the mountains are theirs too. I should have known better and so, they will learn when I am done with them, should have they. This is my domain. Like the Noble Savages, I will not suffer its contamination. I am as irascible as that jealous, fractious old Jehovah God of the Jews and Christians, and will have no other masters before me, as the miners discovered.

Six years ago, I had been here two years then, I returned from my annual trip to Portland for winter supplies. I arrived at the pass in the afternoon and camped for the night, not only to watch the trail behind me for a day or two and assure myself that no one had followed me, but also because I had seen storms playing about in that vicinity and feared the narrow and winding precipitous trail into my valley might be somewheres washed out and so too dangerous at night for a fully loaded horse. The next day I reconnoitered on foot and made some repairs before returning to my horse, and the day after that descended without incident and put up my stores. That night, tho I was tired, I sat in front of my cabin to watch the stars come out, for they have been my bosom companions for three quarters of a century and I was glad to be alone with them after my fill of humanity for the year.

I thought I had dozed and was dreaming when I first heard the voice, but Harry had heard it too for his head and hackles rose and he let out a low growl. I did not blame him for missing the spoor of an intruder, for even as I had seen no trace of anyone's entrance, so too could I not expect Harry to detect a week old trail on a stony path that had been rained on. The wind shifted and the voice faded, but we had heard enough and were on our way without further ado.

Harry preceded, I followed. An hour later tho it was but a twenty minute walk by day, we saw the light of a fire and heard two voices. How they had found their way to my valley I cannot say. They had tho, and luckily for me had taken the left hand path to my small gold mine, else they should have found my cabin first and no doubt despoiled it. They had taken up residence in a rude lean-to I had built there. Two horses and a mule that we avoided were hobbled in the small meadow where I let Duke wander free when I am digging. Their fire, too big for my likes, was placed behind a boulder that hid the men also, but I could see by its light a body lying on the ground. We crept forward silently over the loose tailings. And just as I could tell the body was a woman who had been tied to stakes, the men laughed and one of them rose and approached her.

I have known many women, but never have I had to tie one to stakes to have my way with her, and believe that no man should, for it is wrong. Repulsed, I watched as he undid his trousers and knelt at her side. Then I waited until he covered her and shot him thru from the rear, where I have neither before nor since shot a man, but he deserved no less. The second man tried to flee, but Harry was on him before he could run three steps, and him I finished by breaking open his head with my rifle, which I did not bother to reload for he was not worth a cartridge.

The woman was a red Indian, as I saw when I rolled the corpse off her. They had taken her from a tribe that I knew lived in the foothills, and had used her badly. I loosed the thongs from her wrists where they had cut thru her skin and carried her into the light so I could tend to her, but was too late for she had been beaten and cut open and abused about her privates, and died without a word.

"A noble creature, man," said I to Harry, and in my fury kicked the one I had clubbed to death. "We are better off without him."

I let them lie there that night. The next day I cleansed and laid out the woman in the open in the manner of her tribe, and paid her honors, for I was ashamed of what my kind had done to her and wished her spirit peace. That done, I led the horses and mule out of the valley and set them loose some distance from the pass. Finally, after the flies and bugs had crawled on them and laid their eggs, I dumped the men and all their belongings including two good revolvers and a decent saddle into a shaft that someone had dug long before I found the valley, and covered them over with tailings. It was a fitting burial, for I wanted no man to find them or their bones, or touch the things they had owned.

And now I will play with Andrew awhile for he is awake and frisky and running up and down my arm and exploring in my hair and beard, which tickles me and makes me laugh, which is a rare sound for this cabin. Tonight I will throw out my baited chunks of meat for the gluttons to eat. All the better if the souls of the men whose bones rest in that old shaft reside in the gluttons, as is possible, for they deserve to die again, and a slower death than their first.

January 11

Damn the gluttons to hell, for they must laugh at me and suppose I exist for their sustenance and amusement! I threw out their horse meat last night and they ate it, but like a careful man dining on fish, picked out the bones and left them lying like glistening bent bows atop the soiled snow. I confess they have me at my wit's end, for I cannot say how a glutton can know a man's mind as these must, but not a man a glutton's as I do not. I would shoot them and have done with it, but they are wily and take care not to be seen.

But enough of gluttons, for the thought of them only angers me. I have let them get the upper hand when I meant to continue David's tale.

I have three newspaper articles here that I have read many times about Chas. Darwin, an Englishman. One decries his Theory of Evolution as heretical because it teaches that man is descended from monkeys, which to me is no more patently ridiculous than that a man's soul might derive from a buffalo or upon his death take up residence in a flea. Another is equally ardent in its espousal of this theory and avers that creation is creation however it came about and that God is powerful enough to work His wonders in any manner as strikes His fancy. The third explains this theory by showing how a species adapts to its environment thru the increased longevity of its members best fitted to that environment. I will take issue with neither of the first two, for I have learned that fish will stop breathing water sooner than reason will prevail against faith. But as to the third, I have observed that the process goes two ways and that the environment adapts to fit its component parts. Anyone who does not believe that need only visit some of the southwestern deserts that were once lush but became parched and sere and populated with snakes and lizards after the prospectors exterminated the native predators and, when they died or departed for richer diggings, left behind their burros to breed like rabbits.

Such was the case with the rituals of the Assumption of Culpability and the Gesture of Propitiation, and every other aspect of Home's society and religion. Each was adapted so widely by the time David was a boy that the wild savages who were left in those parts had grown disgusted with their Noble counterparts and gave them a wide berth, the more so because the Guards had become more than a match for them.

The election of the victims had changed considerably over the years. From Jack and Ralph the choice passed to the Conclave of Adepts and the Preeminent One, until one year a young man who was a fanatic stepped forward and became the first Aspirant. The Noble Savages approved of this and rapidly adapted by jointly exerting pressure on one young man and one young woman each year to volunteer, and in return by treating them like a king and queen until the day they died, which honor became vied for among the best young people of the best families.

The annual victims were by then called the Scapeweed Goat and his Ewe, and tho 'scapeweed was still the primary ingredient in the Liquor of the Aspirants, Ralph and his students had modified its effects by adding other compounds to it, partly as a solution to the problem that arose when, instead of the traditional single candidate, two or more fanatics declared themselves Aspirants. A moss that grew in shaded glens and contained an irrevocably addictive ingredient was added. A parasitic gall on milkweeds was discovered to be an aphrodisiac, and it was added. Yet another herb, introduced late in the season, caused suppurating sores that mimicked the spots once painted on.

The season began with the Blessing of the Aspirants on the night of the first full moon midway between the winter and summer solstices, or the first day of spring. The self elected Aspirants, twenty years of age and in robust health, arrived at the meeting hall dressed in breech clouts and painted in gay colors and wearing garlands of holly in their hair. When they had declared their intentions and the assembled Noble Savages had accepted them, the Preeminent One bestowed his blessing on them and in a moving ceremony gave them their first taste of the Liquor of the Aspirants.

Then followed the Feast of Fecundity, or First Feast, which

mimicked the spring rites of the ancient Greeks. No other event occasioned such gaiety. Everyone who could possibly attend filled the streets and environs of New Rousseau. Whole pigs were roasted, and bullocks and deer. The Adepts prepared casks full of a mild infusion of 'scapeweed, which on that one night was permitted, and the common folk drank unrestrainedly of this Drink of Pleasure, which caused them to dance and cavort licentiously until dawn, which was the signal for them to return to their homes and labors.

Not so the Aspirants. To them all things were allowed, and neither man nor woman could touch them in anger or injure them in any way. They could roam the valley at will, save they must return to the great meeting hall to replenish their potion, of which they were allowed at one time only enough to fill a small vial fashioned from an acorn shell. They could copulate with any woman they desired, tho some men denied them their wives and daughters by hiding them. They could eat at any man's table and take of his possessions anything they should desire, and thus they indeed reigned like kings for a time. The time was not long tho, for each in his addiction feared his fellows would consume his share of the potion and began to plot against them. Within a month or two one reigned supreme and the others were dead by his hand, and their bodies slept in a place reserved for them called the Field of Honor while their souls, it was thought, passed into the bodies of a kind of shiny black bird that ate of the 'scapeweed seed when it was ripe, and sang and flew about drunkenly for a week thereafter.

I have said that one of the ingredients was an aphrodisiac, and tho the Aspirants were denied some women, many more freely offered their favors, for the Aspirants' potency was renowned. Some women lay with them once or twice out of curiosity or amusement. Others lay with one long enough to be got with child, which was an honor if he had not taken too much of the drug, for then the child was apt to be a monster which had to be destroyed, or born dead. Some few others became obsessed with the remaining Aspirant, and because he no longer moved about the valley but remained near the source of his pleasure, became his only consorts. This too was destructive, for a certain small portion of the drug entered them thru the Aspirant's bodily fluids. Because one woman was always addicted more readily than the others, either by a natural inclination or by virtue of lying with him more often, she likewise became jealous and suspicious and eliminated her rivals in the same manner as the Aspirant had. The day after she became his only consort, Acolytes ran thru the valley declaring that the Scapeweed Goat and his Ewe were chosen, and announcing the Feast of the Assumption of Culpability, or Second Feast, which was celebrated three nights later.

Full half the summer remained by that time and, due to the great amount of work required to tend the crops and fill their stores for the winter, the Noble Savages' attention drifted away from the Scapeweed Goat and his Ewe. Heavily affected by the drug, for the Ewe could then drink of it, they passed their days eating and sleeping and copulating. Their every need was met without question. The Adepts supplied their drugs. Each household was taxed for offerings of leafy green foods and carrots and onions, which they consumed in quantity, and especially of sides of bacon, for they craved the fried fat of pork and ate prodigiously of it.

The Noble Savages' attention returned to the Scapeweed Goat and his Ewe as the days shortened and the nights turned crisp. Then if the harvest was bountiful the people bestowed gifts and offerings on the sacrificial pair, but if the harvest was poor they grumbled and the Acolytes whose task it was to collect the offerings of food were put to the test. And so it was that when the harvest moon filled, the people gathered in the natural depression under Discovery Promontory and there, watched over by the Face of God, celebrated the Feast of the Gesture of Propitiation, or Third Feast, during which they ate the same food as the Scapeweed Goat and his Ewe, save those two were fed the sacramental Potion of Expiation that released them from their travail. In their dying throes, according to the harvest and the mood of the Noble Savages, they were lauded with tender cries of joy and gratitude or excoriated with surly oaths and imprecations. The lengthy annual ritual ended the next day when they were interred in a special spot in the Field of Honor with their predecessors. The next morning the rest of the Noble Savages returned to their homes to prepare for winter.

K had passed her water and fallen asleep and David and I had finished our small supper when he reached that point in his tale, and stopped abruptly and sat staring into the fire.

My bones were chilled by the barbarity of this murderous custom, but I did not wish to condemn him or his people, and chose my words carefully. "A terrible end," said I. "Not one I should wish for myself or any of mine."

"Nor I, J" said he in a whisper. "Nor I."

"Then I am glad you did not," said I in all sincerity and hoping he would talk more, for I feared the silence of the night. "Tho it sounds as if you 'scaped by only a hair's breadth."

"Nay. By the breadth of my great-grandfather's teaching. Ralph had been the Preeminent One since Jack's death and would have given the position to another had he been allowed. Tired of his responsibilities, he had withdrawn from as many as he could and become a solitary by the time I was a boy. I was the only person Ralph had loved for many years, I think, and he took me to his bosom as no other. We sat for hours beside the lake in the summer and in front of a warm fire in winter while he told me the history of the Noble Savages. He had been proud, in years past, of his discovery of the Face of God in the escarpment below Discovery Promontory and of the part he played in founding a new religion. Bogus tho it was, it served the Noble Savages well and kept their society whole and hale. So much so that he had come to believe in it himself until the Aspirants and Ewes took to killing each other off like fleas, he would say, crushing an imaginary flea between his two cracked and thickened thumb nails. 'No, lad,' he warned me over and over again. 'Say naught of this to thy father or any other man, for they have all become fanatics and are dangerous. But do not forget,' he would add, and pat me on my knee, 'never forget that only a fool becomes either an Aspirant or a Scapeweed Goat, for they exist only to act as a drug on the people.' But I was only a boy of eight or nine when he said these things to me, and tho I loved and revered him, I thought him a doddering old man who spoke nonsense because everything else I had ever learned taught me that the Universal Infinitude was the One True God. And had I not seen His face looking into my soul from the rock that was His abode on earth?"

Ralph, also called the Ancient One by the other Noble Savages, died when David was barely ten. His father and grandfather before him were Adepts, and his mother the daughter of an Adept. So it was that he became an Acolyte shortly after his fourteenth birthday and entered the seven years of his apprenticeship. Twice before, an Acolyte had become an Aspirant, and there had been some who urged David to do so when he came of an age but, with Ralph's warning echoing distantly in his ears, he spoke eloquently of following in his forebears' footsteps and avoided the honor.

David had talked to me off and on for three days, but that was the first time he had referred to any doubts, and he was subdued when he continued his account. At first, tho he had heeded its warning, he rebelled against and denied the nagging voice inside him. After he was installed as an Adept, he donned his mantle of red and blue feathers and went around the countryside from household to household answering questions of faith and judging minor matters of contention. He stood at his father's side during the Announcement of the Aspirants' Intent and clicked his tongue five times in approbation as the 'scapeweed was given and accepted. That night during the Feast of Fecundity he knew for the first time the woman he loved, and a week later he and she cut all the hair off their bodies as was the custom for Adepts and their wives to be, and were married by his father. That summer he and the other two new Adepts watched over and filled the needs of the Scapeweed Goat and his Ewe. Late in the fall they were initiated into the secrets of the Potion of Expiation, and on the night of the harvest moon accompanied the Scapeweed Goat and his Ewe down the ramp into the amphitheater that had been built around the natural depression at the base of Discovery Promontory, administered the potion, and signaled to the assembly its efficacy. They then withdrew from the sight of the Face of God into the woods to purge and purify themselves with emetics during the celebration of the Feast of the Gesture of Propitiation, or Third Feast.

All this time Ralph's voice whispered in David's ear, but he would not be touched by it. And then one night in the following spring, a week after the Feast of Fecundity, his wife called the midwife, for her time was due. Two hours later, after mother and child were cleansed, he stood by his wife's couch and saw she was well. Then when the midwife withdrew for the first viewing, as was the custom, he knelt and pulled aside the cover.

"And beheld my son, naked at my wife's breast," said he, his voice trembling. "My heart filled and joy flowed from my eyes like a woman's, for I had never seen anything of greater beauty. And then spake Ralph's voice again, and I could not close my ears to it, for he bade me consider my son a score of years hence, when he mought well drink of the Liquor of the Aspirants. And that was the last moment in my life that I knew true joy, or aught of peace."

January 14

A man in his right mind can sustain anger and hatred for only a short time if he sits out of doors on a quiet summer night, and as my eyes were drawn to the magnificence of the heavens, those emotions drained from me and left me drowsy. K slept soundly after her purging and David had fallen asleep immediately after closing his eyes, for he was tired after five and a half days of almost ceaseless effort. The night was peaceful with a gently cooling south breeze and the sweet songs of insects and night birds without any interruption to warn of intruders or impending danger. So when the great Orion reached the zenith and I woke David and quit my watch, I lay down on the ground apart from the fire and slept, and did not wake until I heard my wife cry out.

Dawn had come some time before, and the sun had risen above the hills. At once alert, I jumped up and ran to my wife's side where David had just arrived, and discovered her clutching her belly and writhing in agony even as she gasped for breath.

"The child," said David. "Build thou the fire and I will tend to her."

Frightened and slow as a stupid ox, I stood fixed to the spot and stared down at her.

"Fetch thou water too. And put on as much as thou canst to boil!"

My wife's agony abated for a moment, and she opened her eyes and found mine, and clutched my hand. "My water has broke and I cannot stop him, J. Please God, but I am sorry I cannot hold him in me."

Her small hand in mine and the anguish in her voice touched me to the quick, and I knelt at her side and brushed her hair from her brow where it had stuck in the sweat. "There will be others," said I. "Do not worry, for we must save you."

"Thou art wasting time," said David, and took my arm to lift me. "The fire, man, and quickly!"

"Do not leave me, dear J!" cried my wife, and clenched her teeth and groaned.

"The fire, man, yourself," said I, and shook off his hand. "I will tend to my own wife's lying in."

David's chest swelled and his shoulders tensed. "Thou art a fool," said he in a voice filled with contempt. "I tell thee I know some little of these things."

"And you are a dead man," said I, pulling my revolver from my waistband and touching it to his belly, "if you do not see to the fire and the water too this instant. For I tell you, I have done this before and will see to my own wife's lying in."

The color rose in David's face, for he was an Adept and not wont to suffer any common man to speak to him in that manner or threaten him with any weapon, but at last he shrugged and pushed away my revolver with his hand and went toward the fire. I watched him but a second, then laid down my gun and turned again to my wife.

I have read in newspapers that many women now give birth in hospitals, but we were country folk and prepared to do for ourselves. Between her pangs I set to work, first at washing her well, then passing my knife thru the fire and finding a piece of string for the cord. Soon enough I had done what I could, and so sat by her side and held her hands and soothed her with tender words, for tho she was strong and well built for bearing children, she was also weakened by the poison and frightened because this was her first and she feared it would be lost.

No man who has ever attended a lying in can call any birth easy, but this was easier than most, with neither tear nor undue bleeding. Whether it was by the poison or her natural inclination I know not, but her pains increased rapidly, so that she and the water David had put on the fire were ready at the same time. And when once the baby started out he was expelled faster than I have ever seen, and he lay in my hands within half a minute after his head crowned.

Such a frail little thing he was! He was mostly head, and his skin was deeply wrinkled and purple. He had all his parts and was perfectly formed but was emaciated in the extreme, so I think he could not have weighed two pounds. Tho I had never seen such a small baby live and did not think he could, I cleansed his nose and mouth and held him up to breathe into his mouth, and to my surprise he made a squall and breathed, but only once and then expired.

"J? J?" said my wife, for she could read our loss in my face.

"You must rest," said I. "You must finish, and then I will take care of him."

Numbed, I went about my job like a mechanic. I cut the cord and tied it tho there was no need. I washed him well and laid him in a bark cradle lined with moss that David had improvised on the spot. I set aside the after birth and cleansed my wife and covered her, and then sat down at her side with our child in my hands so she might see him as she wished.

My wife's eyes filled with tears as she gazed on him and touched his tiny head with her fingertips. "Oh, J, I did not know this could hurt so very much. Are you angry with me?"

"No, my darling K" said I. "It is not your fault, but of the poison on the bee that stung you, and of the man who threw it."

"Oh J," said she, weeping bitterly and kissing his tiny face all over. "Tell me what kind of man would throw such a monstrous instrument to kill an innocent babe?"

"A savage," said I, not remarking on the Guards or their so called nobility, for she would not have understood. "But we will talk on that another time. For now you must sleep and gain your strength, and I will lay him to his rest."

And so we laid our hands on him together and baptized him

with water and prayed for his soul. Tears ran from my wife's eyes and she averted her head when I rose and walked away from her. No burden had ever been heavier. I took with me our shovel and carried him some distance up the valley to a slight hummock beside a narrow brook that ran into the main stream. There, where he could be alone and rest in peace with the sweet and gentle sound of tinkling water to soothe him, I dug a small grave and gave my son the only kiss he should ever have from his father, and then with trembling hands gently covered him with his only blanket, the warm and aromatic earth.

My wife was asleep when I returned. David sat with his back to her by the fire, where he had gone to give us our privacy. "Asleep," said I, and sat by him. "It is hard on a woman."

"And on a man too."

"Yes. On a man too," I agreed, and added, for I was embarrassed, "Will you forgive me for pointing my gun at you?"

His smile was the gentle one I recalled from better times. "If thou wilt forgive me for snapping at thee like a termagant, aye." He poured and handed me a cup of coffee by way of amends. "I should have understood thee better."

"And I you. In truth, my argument was with another who is not here, and those who sent him. But I will find them if you will show me the way."

"And leave thy wife alone?"

Our loss had addled my senses, and I had forgot my earlier pledge to be grateful if my wife survived. "You are right, hard tho it is not to seek them out," said I. More like my self again, I sipped at my coffee and only then noted the pile of hemp at his feet, and pointed at it. "What is that?"

"A preparation."

"A preparation? It is my one long rope!"

"Aye," said he. "And now thrice as long."

"But only a tenth as strong."

"Still ten times stronger than we need."

Amazed, I stared at him and shook my head. "You must be mad!"

"If preparation be madness, then I am mad." Before I could respond, he nodded solemnly toward the east. "I know the Guards and their methods well, for I lived among them for ten years and can feel them in my bones. I tell thee, J, they are coming. And are not far off."

January 28

I have always had a good memory. I could tell you that I was a lobsterer in Maine in the summer of 1858, and could to this day point out to you the best spots to haul in a catch along the piece of shoreline that I worked. I could relate to you every step of my way over the years thru New Hampshire and New York and Pennsylvania and Ohio, then down thru Kentucky and Tennessee, with a sharp left east to the Atlantic Coast and south and west again along the Gulf Coast to Texas, then north thru Oklahoma Territory and Colorado, where I almost stayed, but that is neither here nor there. I could trace my meandering steps across Utah and Nevada, lead you thru the mountains to the Golden Gate and the Barbary Coast, where I lived with green goods artists, gamblers, thimble riggers, pimps, and con game promoters, not to speak of the madams and the girls who were their commodity. I could show you the sights and where I built my fires after I pointed my toes and followed my nose toward Polaris. I was a peripatetic, working and reading and drawing my round about way across the country as it grew from a fledgling to a mighty nation, all the way to these mountains where at last I found peace and solitude. Why it is, then, that memory suddenly coshes me alongside my thick skull mystifies me. I have often thought of our son and of my wife and our life together. But never as much as during the last few weeks.

Andrew says that I have been running from them all these years and that they finally caught up with me, and I am forced to face the possibility that he is right.

I cannot remember a more unsettling time in my life. I do not understand myself, and have become as much a stranger to myself as I have always taken care to be to others. Ever the itinerant, I fiercely protected my secret identity during the many years I lived side by side with mankind. Only during the last eight in my valley have I been able to relax my guard and find contentment and serenity. What then wrought this change? The unrelenting cold and the depth of the snow? The gluttons who have become my personal devils? I think not. Rather, the reluctant suspicion that this may be my last winter on earth, and that I must make my peace with whatever powers there be.

That is ironical because I had always thought I had made my peace, which shows you how wrong a man may be.

I have drawn my wife in her every mood and in every piece of clothing she owned and wore and in the many kinds of light a day or night may bring, or shadow cast. Endlessly have I imagined in ink and charcoal my son as he might have looked in his youth and manhood. I have sketched a thousand pictures of Old Tige asleep in the sun or sprawled in the shade. Numberless renderings of our valley as it appeared during our days there hang in a thousand homes across the continent. I have thought and thought on those days and never come to this pass.

In another burst of wisdom Andrew says it is the words. Again, he is possibly right, for I have noticed a difference in drawing a picture and committing words to paper. Pictures are like light and shadow in which secrets may hide. Words are like stones that lie on the ground and bruise a man's bare feet as he walks over them. Duke did not understand that, being a stupid beast of a horse. Nor did Harry, God rest his soul if he had one, tho he was smarter by far. Only Andrew, who I have learned to listen to. There is an intelligence behind those beady little eyes. Not a great intelligence, I believe, for he is only a mouse after all, but a kernel of one, and a whole stalk of corn lies in a kernel as every man knows, else he should not plant them.

And this is the kernel. The Devil was walking up and down on the face of the earth and regarded God's servant Job, and took Job's seven sons and three daughters and every other thing he had, but Job surrendered neither his faith nor the good fight and was rewarded. And I? I have been visited with the vicissitudes of life, as has every other man, and have had not one one thousandth the strength of Job, for I lost my faith as fast as a lily of the field does its petals. Compared to me, a mustard seed has faith to strew about the countryside like a prodigal son spending his birthright, and enough left over to move a mountain from here to there. I have poured the water and stirred the dust and made the mud that I have wallowed in, and being covered over with mud, am not a pretty sight.

And this kernel too, which he whispered in my ear from his nest in my hair while I was pissing in the snow. The gluttons are demons and devils come to haunt and taunt me, and I must be rid of them if I am to find peace again. So if piss may form a small hole in the snow, could not buckets of hot water form a larger one? Accordingly, I have spent two weeks hard at work building a trap in which, should I catch one, I might shoot and kill a glutton.

I began by heating and dumping water to form a hole some ten feet deep and lined with ice. The hole made, I saw at once that no glutton would be fool enough to jump in so I might shoot him, but that I must be cagey. To that end I sewed a canvas bag and filled it with stones from my hearth, then played with strings until I had one just strong enough to hold it and a haunch of horse meat well tied together without breaking. This I hung from a sturdy bough, and under it melted another hole like the first, and over the hole constructed a roof. The roof is strong enough to sustain a glutton's weight, but should that glutton leap and catch his prize, beast, meat, and stones will fall and plunge thru that fragile roof and the prize will be mine, for it will be but a simple matter to run outside, throw a torch into the hole, and shoot the glutton before he can dig himself out. Then one more glutton and one more devil will be vanquished.

We will see then how intelligent gluttons may be, and who exists for whose amusement. It is only a matter of time.

One thing I was right about, and more. Andrew is a much better companion than a horse or even, I am sorry to say, Harry, for he eats very little, and my supplies are holding out. So however much I have feared this may be my last winter on earth, I may also still hope that I will reach the hundred years I had planned on, and will not give up the ghost without a fight.

January 29

A man is little given to straight thought when he has just lost a son and when his wife lies in peril on the uppermost rail of the thin fence that separates life and death. Little surprise then, when a minute after I had demanded angrily to be taken to the Guards, I immediately changed the tune I sang and as angrily refused to believe that the Guards should bring themselves to me.

"But that is impossible," I informed David.

"I beg thy pardon?"

"You yourself said the one I wounded died."

"So I did. But also that he might very well have told the others where to find us."

"No," said I, and dashed my cup to the ground. "We are safe, I tell you. Safe!"

David's voice was calm, but he kept a wary eye on my revolver. "Thou art deluded, J, and must listen to me."

"Safe, damn you!" I had taken so many blows during the past six days that one more of such magnitude was beyond my capacity to bear. Half mad, I sprang to my feet and would have pulled my revolver for the second time that morning had not K called my name. Forgetting David on the instant, I ran and dropped to my knees at her side only to discover she had been dreaming and cried out in her sleep.

David knew my mind better than I did, for when I returned all downcast, he waited for me to slump onto the keg I was using as a chair and handed me a fresh cup before speaking. "I know thy anguish, J," said he in that gentle manner he had. "For I too have lost a son, and a wife and daughters as well. But a true man o'errides his anguish, else he is crushed and sinks even deeper into dark despair."

"You are no longer an Adept," said I with a sneer, for I did not relish being patronized, "so do not become one again on my account and preach to me."

"Thou art right," said he with a smile. "I had better speak of the Guards, and how we might defeat them."

"If they come," said I, giving in a little.

"I will gladly be the butt of thy derision if they do not. But if they do, thou must needs know I cannot save thee by drawing them off, for they will first believe thou art a threat to Home and will second demand a reckoning for the two of them you killed. Thou wilt beg to die before they finish with thee, for they have their ways."

"I have my own ways and will beg with this," said I, patting my revolver, "and we will see who finishes who."

By way of answer David pulled my separated rope from the bucket he had set it in to soak, and began to tie off one end of each strand to a post we had set before the fire.

"Well?" said I. And as there was again no answer, I followed him as he unraveled the strands while walking toward the nearest tree. "Surely a man with a gun is more than a match for a man without one."

"Two Guards have been killed by gunfire in these past five years. They have killed ten times that number of Outsiders armed with guns in that same time. They no more fear guns than thou wouldst an ox."

"Ha!" said I. "They are like red Indians then, and strike from ambush."

"Sometimes, aye." He stretched the lines taut and tied them so they should dry straight. "Sometimes too one stands before a man and challenges him to his face. I have not seen this trick played but have seen them practice it and watched them bury men who had wielded guns, which served them no better than a wish upon the wind. Most often tho, they attack by night, and stealthily from several directions. We are but two men, J. They will be as many as nine but no less than six, for they travel in threes and with double the number they think they will need. So wilt help me or no? Four days for the wounded man to return, three for his avengers to make their way here. Seven days in all, and less if he met a band on his way. We must needs finish today, for they will be watching us by morning."

I confess he had shaken my confidence and made me feel more like a pup still wet behind the ears than a grown man. "You know a lot for a priest, an Adept," said I, of a sudden suspicious of him.

"More than either thou or they may guess, which may yet be our salvation." He laughed and clapped me on the shoulder.

"Come. Axes and broad knives first. I will talk whilst we work, and satisfy thy every question."

I was young. I had never been on a river at its flood, never been on a train racing without brakes down a mountainside. Never had I run into a barn full of burning hay with beams falling about my ears to pluck a mother and her two babes from certain death. I had not yet been trapped on a cliff with a war party of raiding Indians racing toward me on fleet ponies and my only salvation a river an hundred feet below. I had yet to face those perils, but I learned on that day that when fear churns a man's stomach and soaks his palms with sweat he must hold on or brave the flames or leap according to the circumstances, or simply perish.

My father had told me that more than once but I had been a boy, and had not listened to him.

January 31

The gluttons grow bolder, for which I am for the first time thankful. I heard them snuffling around my trap last night, which prevented me from pursuing these memories. I sat by the door with gun in hand until late. Andrew says they will want two more nights to build up their confidence in the frail roof over the hole, and I say but one. I have promised him one of my precious dried berries if I am wrong. He is quite at home with me now, so I have put a stick against his biscuit tin for him to go in and out when he pleases. I know such a thought is an aberration engendered by solitude, but I am convinced he reads every word I write as he sits on my left wrist and watches with his beady eyes as the words flow onto the paper. He will not talk about it tho, so perhaps I am wrong.

David's son grew, as sons will. He was a fair lad, lighter than David and some pudgier, tho he later outgrew that and became slim as a reed. After him came three daughters, and a year after the last was born David's wife died a horrible death when a bucket of fat she was rendering spilled on her and scalded her down the front. The three girls were sent to other families to be raised and there were those who wanted his son, but David would not relinquish him and kept him at his side as he strode the outer reaches of Home.

David remembered the next five years with his son as the happiest in his life, which I well understand since I spent most of those same boyhood years of my life in the wilderness with my father. But he had something my father thankfully lacked, which was the quiet voice in him that grew louder every spring as the Feast of Fecundity neared and the willing young men stepped forward to drink the Liquor of the Aspirants. And as the voice grew, so did a dangerous idea: that when his son was old and strong and fast enough, they would leave Home together and become Wanderers.

The Preeminent One would have stripped him of his feathered mantle had he guessed David's thoughts. However dangerous the idea tho, the act itself was ten times more so, for no Adept could ever hope to escape the Guards if they pursued him. And then one day David was summoned before the Conclave of Adepts and told that he would thenceforth minister to the Guards. His first thought was to refuse because his son could not accompany him, but a blinding light struck him even as he opened his mouth, and he said instead that he did not deserve the honor but would do his best etc. A month later he installed his son in the home of a trusted friend and went to serve the Guards, and secretly learn their ways the better to evade them when the time was ripe.

An eighteen year old in his prime may easily master feats that a man above thirty can learn only thru long hours of practice and some little pain. David did nothing at first save

85

watch and listen. Only when his duties took him from camp to camp was he free to put his plan to action. Home exceeded forty miles in length, and its circumference as measured from Guard camp to Guard camp was over an hundred miles. The camps lay one each at the north and south ends, and two each on the east and west sides, and it was as he walked from one to the other that he practiced the art of the Guards.

David had been given a hardy constitution from birth, and ten years of walking thru the countryside had strengthened his legs. His wind tho was short, so he improved it first. By the end of his second year his practice was to walk out of one camp and disappear down the path toward the next and then, by running up and down the hills and back and forth along the trail, cover three times the distance between the camps in the same time it took any other man to walk. In that same time he learned what a man might pick and eat to sustain himself while traveling so he needn't burden himself with food, and how to walk in cold water without numbing his feet and mind, and cross a torrent without being swept off his feet. He learned the tricks of hiding his sign too, and tho his skill did not equal that of the Guards, he dared hope he could confuse them long enough to allow him and his son to reach Civilization and a safety in numbers. Most important of all, he noted carefully the comings and goings of the Traders, and by conversing with them in a jocular manner learned round about the directions to the nearest towns of Civilization, and what one might expect to find in them.

His ministry to the Guards began shortly after the Feast of Fecundity when his son was ten, and he planned to leave Home on the night of the same feast four years later when his son was fourteen. To this end he insidiously turned his son against becoming an Acolyte, and planted in him by devious means and sly suggestions a dissatisfaction with Home in the hopes that he should leave willingly when the time came. He would have succeeded too, he told me as a distant look came into his eyes and he paused in his labors, were it not for a pair of disasters that foiled his plans and turned the Noble Savages onto a macabre and horrific path.

The first disaster was man made. On the morning after the Feast of Fecundity of the year before he planned to leave, an itinerant drummer opening a new territory for himself escaped detection by the Guards, whose vigilance at that season was relaxed, and wandered into Home. Worse luck on top of bad, a heavy rain that morning washed out his tracks, so he was given a full week to ply his trade before anyone moved to stop him.

A woman wearing a shell comb in her hair led to his downfall. A simple peasant, she had gone to North Town on trading day and wandered unchecked half the morning before a horrified Adept noticed her adornment, snatched it out of her hair, and demanded to know how and where she had got it. Immediately a runner was dispatched to the Guards, who found the drummer that afternoon asleep under his wagon halfway down the western edge of the valley.

Seldom, I imagine, has a drummer had a ruder awakening. Six menacing figures painted with black and gray blotches surrounded him. An imposing man wearing a cape of red and blue feathers asked him questions that, since he believed himself innocent of any wrongdoing, he answered honestly. No, he said, no man had helped him enter the valley. He had simply driven in. Yes, he had traded, he said, and showed them the inside of his wagon, which was half emptied of goods and half filled with the dog and rabbit and bird dolls the peasants made for their children from bone and skin and feathers. He had never seen their like, he explained, and would make a pretty penny on them. His surprise when they slit his horse's throat and set fire to his wagon was short lived, because they then killed him without further ado and threw his corpse into the burning wagon. The next day the Guards dug a pit in which they buried the ashes, and then set out to confiscate all the goods they could find, for the Preeminent One had deemed them abominations and ordered their destruction.

Their task was as far from simple as the Atlantic Ocean is from the Pacific, for the marvels the drummer had imported had become treasures no less valuable than the crown jewels of England. The news of the Preeminent One's edict and the Guards' intentions spread faster than ripples through water, and the peasants, who were simple, honest folk, learned as rapidly to lie. Yes, they had heard of an Outsider, but he had not stopped at their farm. Yes, they traded with him, but only for some little things he called buttons, while all the time the lace and the fans, the shell combs and the steel hair pins and the gaily colored playing cards and the boxes that sang tinkling songs lay hidden in holes in trees or other secret places.

The Adepts and Guards were furious, for they had rarely been lied to before. Some peasants were beaten and one was killed by accident, but the conflagration set by the drummer far outshone the puny fire that destroyed his wagon and poor self, and raged unchecked. All too soon the treasures spread thru Home. A small glass mirror was worth a cock and six hens, a deck of playing cards a good pair of breeding sheep or a sow. A music box was worth a cow and a calf, two a bull. No class was immune. A Guard was executed when his superiors discovered he had given a comb to his wife. An Adept was made a peasant after an irate husband learned his wife had accepted a piece of lace in return for her favors. Most dangerous of all, some of the Noble Savages, who came to be called Civilizers, began to wonder what other marvels Civilization had to offer and to speculate whether the time had come for the Noble Savages to take the Truth of the Universal Infinitude to the civilized nations. So great was the furor that the Feast of the Assumption of Culpability was marred by brawls, and a Guard was assaulted and beaten viciously when he tore a button from a woman's vest.

This disaster would have portended the destruction and

downfall of Home had it not been for a second, which was sent by nature. It started at the north end of the valley and took the form of a rust that blackened and killed whole fields of wheat. The news spread quickly, and what began as a trickle of concern soon swelled to a torrent of consternation and fear. Public and private prayers were offered. The peasants, being superstitious, slaughtered chickens and sprinkled the blood over their lands. The rusted fields were burned, and also a swath of good ones across the entire middle of the valley, but the scourge jumped the burned fields as if they were not there and continued its southward march.

The Preeminent One pointed out that the sickness in the wheat followed the path the trader had taken, and deemed it a judgment against the people for desiring, holding, and trading the unclean things of Civilization, and warned that the people would sicken and die if they did not publicly destroy their evil possessions. Immediately scores of combs and buttons and pieces of lace and music boxes and other trinkets were brought to the squares in the towns to be smashed and burned and buried, but the rust was not abated. Before one head of grain could be harvested, the entire crop lay in utter ruin.

David thought the schism between the Civilizers and the rest of the Noble Savages would flare anew and with increased ferocity once it was seen that Home's winter stores would be slim beyond any time in memory, but he was wrong. Instead, the disaster ignited a raging inferno of religious fervor that taught the Civilizers to hold their tongues and sent them scurrying for shelter. Men and women prayed in the middle of streets. So many offerings were brought to the Scapeweed Goat and his Ewe that they could not be eaten, and lay on the ground and rotted and raised a great stench and gathered a horde of flies, which too was seen as a judgment.

The greatest disaster of all tho was personal. For when David returned from the camps of the Guards for his lunar visit, he found that his son had been caught up with the rest of the people in their fanaticism and could talk of nothing but his wish, tho he was too young, to be an Aspirant and a Scapeweed Goat, and so give of himself that Home might be freed of its bondage and despair.

February 6

Oh my God, my God! I would speak of disasters, and now one has befallen me. Andrew won his wager and I have given him his berry, but gladly should have paid half my store if neither of us had won, or if I had not been vindictive and concocted a hare brained scheme whose cost I cannot yet tell.

Four nights ago, thinking the gluttons would fall into my trap, I listened 'til I fell asleep by my fire. Three nights ago, I heard a great commotion and howling outside and loosed a cry of triumph. All was ready. I sprang up and thrust the torch I had waiting into the fire. I plucked Andrew from my shoulder where he had been sitting and pulled on my parka, for a gale was howling. I took my gun off the wall and checked its load, and then with torch and gun ran out my door.

The moon was shining and sparkling on the blowing snow, and I saw when I left my porch that the horse meat and bag of stones were no longer hanging from their bough, and that there was a dark circle in the snow where they had fallen thru the roof of my trap.

Elk and deer may be shot easily, and so may bears for all their size unless one be an old and wily grizzle. Grouse and ptarmigan are harder to bag, as antelope may be too these days tho previously they were simple beasts to slay. The hardest of

all animals to kill is the glutton, for tho they are smaller than
Harry was and weigh but half an hundredweight, they are fast
and wily and of so mean a disposition that even wolves and
bears avoid crossing their paths. So would men were the glutton's fur not impervious to frost and hence valuable for hoods
to protect their faces against the cold. He is said to be the
strongest for his size of all the animal kingdom, not counting
the insects. So it was then that I did not run to my trap as a
boy might, but stopped to breathe twice slowly before pushing
a skid I had made of branches close to the hole, for I did not
relish the idea of caving down the side and falling in with him
and being made short work of.

I could hear him inside growling and jumping about, and
could smell him too when I stuck my head over the edge, for
he had exuded his musk copiously in his anger and fear. I had
sharpened the end of my torch to a point so it should stick
upright when I dropped it from a height, and when I did I
confess I drew back, for sound and smell are but petty senses
when compared to the sight of a glutton that is aroused. They
are fearsome creatures, somewhat like a badger but longer and
leaner and more agile, and their claws and teeth are long and
sharp.

This one did not like the fire of my torch. Backing from it
to the wall of his cage, he growled and snapped at it.

"I have got you now, devil," said I, and cocked my gun but
held my shot. "You have eaten and spoiled the last of my meat.
Why are you not laughing now, eh?"

I have long held that a man who baits a dog or a bear is that
much less a man, and that he should not gloat when he has
any animal or other man at a disadvantage or his mercy, for it
is mean and unseemly. I am not proud then that I taunted the
glutton that had given me so much misery, but am glad none
the less, for had I shot him on first sight I believe I should be
dead now.

I was lying on my stomach at the edge of the pit and looking

in when I separated another sound from his. Not yet understanding, I looked over my left shoulder and saw the shadowy
streak of my victim's mate running across the snow toward me,
and grunting as she came.

I was once attacked by a large dog but made short work of
him by plunging my blade into his heart. A glutton tho is as
much like a dog as a sequoia is like an aspen. Both are trees
and made of wood and may be cut down and burned, but that
is where the likeness ends.

I did not know that gluttons were so loyal to their mates or
that they ran so fast, and had but time to roll once away from
the hole before she was on me. How long our battle lasted I do
not know. I remember seeing her fly thru the air at me and
thrusting out my hand to stop her and feeling the jolt when
she hit me and rolled me over in the snow. I remember the
shock of pain as her claws raked my arm and her teeth tore
thru my glove and hand. I remember her stench and her fierce
growls. I remember being shaken the way a rabbit is shaken by
a dog. I remember trying to push her away from me with my
left hand and jamming my gun into her and searching for the
trigger which I had lost and finding it and in the fleeting
second before I pulled it hoping the barrel did not explode in
my face, for it is old and almost shot thru and a .50 caliber
buffalo gun is not designed to be fired at arm's length with its
muzzle blocked.

I do not remember the first time I ever fired a gun and
would not hazard a guess at how many times I have since then.
I remember some shots, like the time I dropped an elk in its
tracks at five hundred yards, or when I brought down two
geese with one round that took off the first one's head and
entered the breast of the second. This shot tho I will remember
if I live to be two hundred and forget everything else. My gun
did not explode, else I should not be here to write this, but the
effect was almost as dramatic. The glutton was killed on the

instant with a hole blown thru her chest and half her back ripped away. As tho kicked by a mule, I skidded backward past my trap as if on a sled. My gun flew up and over my head and was luckily attached to me by my finger else I fear I should not have found it in the darkness.

How long I lay there I do not know, but my first thought after I came to my senses and saw I was alive was to get inside, for I could hear the glutton in my trap trying to dig his way out and I did not wish to be attacked again. My left hand and arm were numb. Holding them against me, I stumbled to my feet, which was not easy in my state, and gathered my gun out of the snow and lurched like a drunkard for the warmth and safety of my cabin. Seldom have I been happier to shut the door behind me and look about me at all my things, for I had feared I would never see them again, nor Andrew, who was peering at me over the edge of his biscuit tin.

I have seen many times when a man is hurt that his face turns white and he sweats and is dizzy so he must lie down, and this is called shock tho no electrical current is applied to the body. Put that same man alone and a numbness may pass thru him, and a certain calm too, for he knows there is no one to help him. And so I gritted my teeth and set to work. Snow had got down my back and up my sleeves, so I shed my parka. My left glove was in shreds, and it I cut away and also my shirt, for I could not bear to draw it over my hand and arm, which had not yet begun to hurt but were bleeding profusely. Wishing first to stop the bleeding, I tore my shirt in strips by holding it down with one foot and bound it tight about my wounds as best I could and poured cool water on it, then hung my arm in a sling I built from the rest of my shirt and dozed off for some minutes in my exhaustion. When I woke, the arm was throbbing and tho I wanted to doctor it, I first built up my fire and filled all my buckets and pots with fresh snow to melt and boil and sharpened my small knife and prepared some cloth for bandages, and the while tried to calm poor Andrew, who was frightened and had lost his wits and ran from one end of my table to the other in a dither.

The bleeding was but an ooze when I removed my bandages to survey the damage. The gashes on my forearm were deep and painful but ran length wise and were not dangerous. My wrist and hand were another matter entirely, for the skin and meat over my wrist hung in shreds held together with clots of blood where she had clawed me, and my hand was crushed where she had bit into me and was swollen to twice its size. Two of the holes her teeth had made were so deep that I could run a probe made of a straightened bucket bail clear thru tho the pain was intense. Altogether my wrist and hand were as much a mess as I have seen in a long life, and tho I wished my wounds away, there was naught to do but set to work.

To begin with, I soaked the whole thing in hot salted water to wash away the blood so I might see what I had to do. Next I scrubbed and scoured it thoroughly with lye soap and fresh water save for in the gouges in the bones of my wrist and in the deep holes in my hand where I could not reach, and that is dangerous, for gluttons are carnivores and carry bits of rotted meat between their teeth and on their claws, which if allowed to remain in a wound must certainly pustulate. Still, I had done my best for the moment, so gave it a good salt water soak and at last poured over it some of the whiskey I had left, which made me faint for some minutes, then wrapped it anew and lay down to rest, for I was done in.

My fire was low when I woke, and it was light outside. Andrew had found his way down the table leg and up the bed leg and was curled in a ball and asleep on my chest. I did not feel bad save that my hand was hot. Hanging it down caused pain and walking more, but a man cannot lie in bed and live so I hung it in my sling and set about my chores.

It is no easy matter to work with one hand, but of course I did. I built up my fire and heated water and the gruel and meat left over from the night before. I went out to piss and bring in wood and on my way inspected the glutton I had killed, which was when I saw it was the female, and discovered too that the male had dug himself out and disappeared. I drank water and ate, for tho my stomach quailed the water leaches impurities from the blood, and food gives strength. At last I doctored my wounds again and soaked them in salt water to draw out the poisons that I feared would putrify my hand if left alone.

That was three days ago. Since then my cabin has been like an Indian bath from the buckets of snow I have melted and boiled to soak my hand and clean my bandages. The swelling has gone down a little, and tho I had begun to think I would overcome this disaster I am now not so sure, for I woke some hours ago during the night with my hand throbbing and with somewhat of a fever, and could not sleep again for the worry so took out my paper and pen. Now I can see light thru my one small window, so day is here and I will begin my regimen of drinking and pissing and eating and soaking all over again, and hope for the best.

February 9

I busy myself during the day getting about, cooking and eating my food, drinking and pissing my water, and doctoring my arm and hand. Much of the night I lie awake both for the fever that comes and goes and for the getting up to piss and drink and piss again, and sleep but fitfully. My wrist and hand look such a fright I cannot believe they belong to me, but they do. Some of the flesh is turning black and I must cut it away. A pox on this winter! Were it summer I could get some maggots on me to keep the dead flesh eaten away and not dwell so constantly on the fear of putrefaction. Andrew wrinkles his nose and turns away in disgust when I tell him about the maggots. He says he would not sit still for a fly to lay eggs on him, and refuses to believe that maggots keep a wound cleaner than anything I have ever seen.

We worked hard that day long cutting saplings and vines and hanging logs under the eaves of my cabin and bringing the wagon bed inside, all the time looking after K and tending her, for she was restless and dreaming, I think, about our son. Our meal was poor that night, namely rice and the last of our crock of sausage patties which we ate because David wanted to use the lard they were packed in. He did not think K's crisis would come before morning, so told me to sleep when the sun went down. I could not tho, for my worries about K and the Guards too, for I had gone full circle and believed they would come, so I moved back to the fire where David was busy melting lard in our large kettle.

"Thou wouldst be thankful in the morning for some sleep," said he when I approached.

"That may be," said I, and asked what he was doing.

For answer he removed his shirt and pants and to my amazement dropped them in the kettle.

"Good God, man! You would eat your clothes?" I asked, only partly in jest.

"Wear them," said he, stirring them about. I looked as disgusted as Andrew did when I told him about the maggots, but David only smiled. "The grease absorbs the poison. I cannot hope to dodge every little bee that flies my way."

"Well then," said I, "I hope you are prepared to stink."

"Better rancid than dead," said he, and pulled out his clothes and hung them to cool. As natural as if he were wearing a full suit, he sat down on the other side of the fire from me and poured us both a cup of broth. "Wouldst hear more of the Noble Savages?"

I have observed that there are three kinds of memory. The first is of things learned, e.g. that the Mississippi River flows into the Gulf of Mexico or that green wood does not burn as easily as cured. The second is of experiences recalled whether they be remote or recent, e.g. the lopping off of my finger or meeting Andrew. The third is of a different order and occurs when one sees and hears an event as if it were happening again. It may be induced by a pipe full of the herb of dreams or by wistful introspection or sometimes slip up on a man by surprise, jogged by some happenstance that calls to mind a distant time and place. Fever too may be its instigator, as I have noted in the past and anew tonight as those long ago events fill my thoughts.

Our valley is so calm that the smoke from our fire rises in a straight line. The thin sliver of moon we can expect that night has yet to rise. The heavy odor of hot lard overwhelms the sweet scent of earth. An owl that lives in a dead cottonwood next to our stream calls now and again. In the background the songs of myriad insects are pierced by the peeping of small frogs and underlaid with the deep, vibrant thrum of the bullfrogs that live sheltered by the cattails growing up stream where the water widens and slows. My fields look so placid, so peaceful and benign in the soft starlight. Beyond them the trees that grow on the distant hills are black and hide mysteries, and I am thinking that were I in the forest I would be at home and feel no mystery, but rather sense it in the emptiness of the open valley.

David is the very picture of elemental manhood. He sits on the ground with his legs crossed, his back straight, and his hands on his knees. He is naked and the meager light from our fire makes his skin glow like copper. He is lean and looks frail, but I note anew how wiry he is and recall his tremendous strength. His face is all angles made the sharper by the combination of the darkness and the firelight. His hair is black and hangs past his shoulders, and shines like adamantine. His voice is soft and low and melodious. I no more listen to him than I do the owl, yet his words sink into me as if he did not speak them with his mouth but shot them from his brain to mine, where they are as indelibly recorded as music I have heard that was impressed on wax drums or poked into metal discs.

There was little David could do about his son's wish to become an Acolyte save listen in despair and return to his duties. His path was unclear. Being separated from his father had left the boy open to the influences of others, and yet David had had to leave him in order to learn the skills that would permit them to become Wanderers and live to tell the tale. He wallowed in his despair for a full year. The summer was difficult because the Guards' vigilance was extreme after they had let the drummer in and the people had blamed them for their woes. The autumn and especially harvest time were agonizing for he could not help but see the light of fanaticism shining in his son's eyes during the Feast of the Gesture of Propitiation. The winter was long and hard for the Noble Savages' stores were meager without their wheat, and the weather was cold and miserable with heavy snows and thick ice and strong winds. His spirits lifted somewhat with spring, but then were dashed when eight Aspirants stepped forward to receive the 'scapeweed, which was the greatest number ever. Six weeks later seven young men lay dead and filled seven fresh graves in the Field of Honor, and his son approved and they were further apart than ever.

It was thought, as time passed, that the sacrifice was pleasing, for the young wheat was a deep, bright green, looked strong, and grew apace. By the middle of the summer tho, the rust appeared again when the heads began to fill out. The people were one day despondent, the next in a frenzy. Prayers were offered. The Traders were consulted and reported no rust destroying the crops of Civilization, but this intelligence was kept from the people. The peasants slaughtered more chickens and again scattered blood, and the practice was imitated by the

Adepts, who sacrificed and burned a fine pair of oxen in a ceremony presided over by the Preeminent One. All went for naught tho, for the rust was not stayed and the crop was again utterly lost save for enough to plant that fall.

The second year of the rust was the same year the Smoke of Retribution was invented. It had long been known that the smoke of a certain vine damaged the lungs. That vine, it was further discovered, exuded an oily milk that when boiled became thick and viscous and burned with a heavy caustic smoke. So it was that cages were built, and in their tops were fitted funnels made of gourds over which were set stone braziers. When the oil was set on fire, the smoke flowed over the edges of the brazier and fell thru the funnel into the cage. When it was breathed, its victim's eyes and lungs burned and he suffered an agonizing death. Three peasants became Wanderers that year, two with their whole families. The two with families soon were caught and subjected to the new invention before the assembled population of North Town and its environs so they should be made an example for the other peasants, but the one man alone escaped, which led to great consternation and a condemnation of the Guards until his body was discovered later in a ravine. His skull was carried back and displayed about Home as a lesson that the Universal Infinitude frowned on Wanderers, but David's faith was so shaken that he was not dismayed. On the contrary, he observed that the poor fellow had merely fallen over a precipice and broken his neck. From him he took his inspiration, for he believed himself a cut above a simple peasant with nary more than his native wit and became determined to escape with his son even if he had to drug him and carry him out on his back. Immediately he set to work at his old regimen and

The male is at my door.

February 10

The glutton was here. I heard him scratching at my door and saw the marks this morning when I went to dump the bucket I piss in at night rather than leave my bed. When I heard him, I loaded my gun and proved my state of mind by shooting at him thru the door tho I know better, for I did him no harm and only deafened myself and sent Andrew into hiding where he remains. I miss him and have strewn some grain on my table top and put out some water, and can only hope he will return.

I thought I would write more again last night but did not because my ears rang so I could not think. Also, I struck my hand on the edge of the table, which made it ache fearsomely. At last I smoked a pipe of the herb of dreams and dozed off in my chair. I do not remember if I dreamed and am thankful for that.

I left David filled with determination and beginning his old regimen, which consumed his time and busied his mind. He built his wind again. He toughened his body by cold swims and fasting. In the spring he diligently practiced the skills the Guards permitted no one outside their number to learn. He watched the young men train with their throwing knives, purloined three and practiced surreptitiously until he could stick them into a tree at twenty paces, and once killed a running rabbit. In like manner he learned to limb walk from tree to tree by using a short rope, and to blend so completely into his surroundings that a deer could approach him without sensing his presence. He stole a small pouch filled with the Wasps of Death and learned to hurl them with great speed and accuracy, and he learned the Weaving Dance by which a man might walk directly to another man who was shooting at him with a gun or bow and arrow or other projectile, and tho he was never able to practice this against weapons as the Guards did, he was confident he would pass the test should the day come.

That it should come was a conclusion he had accepted, for he had become utterly disillusioned and repulsed by the excesses practiced by the Noble Savages. The next year ten young men became Aspirants, one of them for the first time purposely maiming himself by scarifying his arms to show his dedication. The rust returned that year for the third time, which was the more dangerous because the spring had been wet and the corn got in late and was subsequently damaged by borers. That autumn the people reviled the Scapeweed Goat and his Ewe because they had not assumed the burden of the people's sins as they were supposed to, and spat on them when they went forward to lay their offerings around them after they were dead, and went to their homes without any celebration.

Better that the Great Schism had sent the Noble Savages into the embrace of Civilization, David thought, than that they endure the slaughter that followed during the fourth year of the rust. Six more peasants, two with wives and children, and a young Adept became Wanderers that year. Five of the adults and the young Adept were captured and suffered the Smoke of Retribution, and the other three adults were slain as they ran and their heads brought back. Four babes and youths, so cruelly and abruptly orphaned, were put out to new families. That same summer the blood of eleven Aspirants, all maimed, for the practice had been quickly adopted, and of seven young women ran thru the streets of New Rousseau ere the Scapeweed Goat and his Ewe were ensconced in their propitiatory office. The number was calamitous for a population of less than four thousand, but David held his peace and tongue alike when he visited his son, who was the foremost in his class of Acolytes and contemptuous of the slightest criticism brought against the Noble Savages or their ways.

David was aware of the Civilizers' cult that was dedicated to
taking the Truth to the civilized nations, and knew that they
shared his revulsion for the fanaticism of the people, the cor-
ruption of the Truth, and the annual slaughter of the youngest
and best Noble Savages, but being so much absent from New
Rousseau dared trust but one old friend from whom he got
his information. Alone and sick at heart in a small and aberrant
world, among but not one of the Guards, he rose in the morning to don his Mantle of Feathers and lead the dawn devotions.
He taught the Truth to the young Guards and counseled with
them and their elders. He presented himself as an humble
example of diligence and faith, and he deprecated Civilization's
evils even as he extolled the wonders and marvels of the Noble
Savages and Home, with which no people or place might compare. The while, he dissembled with every breath, held to his
regimen, and added to it the exercise of carrying a bag he had
sewn in the shape of a man and filled with dirt to his son's
approximate weight.

If the people thought their sacrifices would alleviate their
troubles they were wrong, for the rust destroyed the wheat for
yet a fourth time. The mood in Home grew uglier than ever.
A rumor that the Guards and Adepts were eating wheat bread
brought in by the traders ran through the valley, and three
Adepts in the countryside surrounding South Town were
stoned and two killed before the stories were proved to be the
work of the Civilizers. The ugliness reached its zenith that
autumn during the Feast of the Gesture of Propitiation. Some
weeks before, a band of rowdies had torn off the shutters on
the meeting hall where the Scapeweed Goat and his Ewe lived,
so they should have no privacy. Not that those two miserable
souls cared, for they had become more animal than human as
the 'scapeweed destroyed all the better parts of their minds.

They ate from the floor what food was thrown there,
munched on whole unwashed onions and carrots and leafy
vegetables and searched thru the debris for what pieces of

bacon they had missed, and grunted like pigs. The rashes that began on their bodies in the late summer had not yet turned to open sores, but none the less drove them mad with itching that came and went at odd times and made them scratch, to the amusement of the watchers.

Worse by far was the effect of the aphrodisiac. Sometimes the man became stiff and accosted the woman who would fight him off and he would moan and cry out in his anguish and at last relieve himself by his hand, which made the watchers laugh. Sometimes the woman became desirous of the man and tried to rouse him by stroking and licking him and displaying herself to him in a lascivious manner, and if he was not aroused she at last used her fingers or relieved herself with one of the large carrots the watchers had brought and thrown to her, and then they would show her their own carrots, which was what they had taken to calling their male members, to arouse her further. David himself saw this sight once and left ashamed of his fellow Noble Savages, for they laughed and pointed at her when to please them she wiggled her private parts with the carrot sticking out of them, but when she was finished, she sat alone and disconsolate in the middle of the floor, her naked body filthy and her hair matted with grease and pieces of rotting food, her eyes staring empty and sad at them like an animal that has been whipped until its spirit is altogether broken.

The Feast of the Gesture of Propitiation was by that time the highest day of the year, on which anger and hope mixed in the people and produced a frenzy of emotion. They were angry with the Scapeweed Goat and his Ewe because they had not averted the rust, and filled with hope that their sacrifice should sway the Infinitude to release them from their travail. In the fourth year of the rust, North and South Town and all the countryside emptied and campfires ringed New Rousseau on the night before the Third Feast. The next evening before the ceremonies began, the Scapeweed Goat and his Ewe were released from the meeting hall and driven with scourges to the amphitheater under the Face of God. Because the people were restless and the occasion so important, for Home's fortunes had sunk so low, the Preeminent One declared a new tradition and decreed that the people be given the Drink of Pleasure, which was before reserved only for the night of the Feast of Fecundity.

The ceremonial dancers were greeted with a roar of approbation. The Administrator, who in recent years had become the Preeminent One's chief secular assistant, praised the people for their great harvest of corn and beans and oats and pigs, and promised that no man or woman or child should suffer from hunger that winter. A respectful hush fell over the assembled people then when the new Adepts administered the Potion of Expiation to the Scapeweed Goat and his Ewe, and continued thru the Preeminent One's sermon, in which he predicted a mild winter and assured them by incontrovertible logic that the Infinitude would bless them and bring wheat bread to their tables by that time the next year. This was applauded loudly by the Noble Savages, for they were disgusted with unleavened bread made from corn.

And then occurred an event of such horror that David related it in a voice so low I had to lean forward to hear.

Always before, the Scapeweed Goat and his Ewe had fallen lifeless during the Preeminent One's sermon, which he ended by eulogizing them and entreating the people to come forward with their offerings. On this night tho, for whatever the reason, the Potion of Expiation did not work, and as chance would have it the Scapeweed Goat and his Ewe were both become aroused during the sermon and she stood with her hands on her knees and her back to him and he entered her, so when the sermon ended they were swaying toward and away from each other and all the while slowly turning from side to side and staring out with wide eyes in fear of the assemblage that faced them.

A great and ominous silence fell over the Noble Savages. The new Adepts were pushed forward to administer more of the Potion of Expiation, but they in their trepidation stopped in terror and could not be made to approach the rutting pair. Still the two continued their futile exercise in what I imagine was an attempt, tho I cannot think they had any understanding of this, to create life at the moment of their death.

David had stood some ways apart from them on the height at the edge of the amphitheater, and his words painted a more vivid picture than I could with brushes and jars of pigment. There beneath him was assembled a throng of almost four thousand souls. Below them, their bodies glistening in the silver moonlight, the sacrificial pair moved in a slow lascivious dance. Save for their moans, which carried on the still air, all else was silent until from somewhere in the throng a voice rose.

"Slay them! Slay them! Slay them!"

Another voice and another joined the first, and before a heart could beat a score of times a monstrous chant rose to become a mindless roar as men and women leaped down from their seats on the terraced walls of the amphitheater and raced across the floor to hurl the carrots and onions and pigs' heads they had brought to place on the offering heap that was meant to hide the corpses of the hapless pair. The Scapeweed Goat was struck first by an onion that broke open one of his sores. He howled in pain and pulled away from his Ewe and would have run but could find nowhere to go. A pig's head struck the Ewe, who cried out and fell and rose again bleeding from her face. The air filled with missiles that struck their flesh and drew their blood until at last, immobilized by pain and fear, the Scapeweed Goat stood straight and howled a terrible scream as his seed spilled from him, and dropped dead by the side of his mate, who had already fallen.

And I will stop for this night on that unhappy note, for my hand is in great pain.

February 15

I came to my senses sometime during these three days past to find Andrew sitting on my knee. He has been sympathetic to my plight and a comfort in my distress, but I would gladly give my gold mine for another human presence. To that end I dreamed that David walked thru my door to succor me with his skills. The dream was so real that I waked with his name on my lips and was sore disappointed. When I think on it tho, I do not see how he could help me lest he could work magic with salt and whiskey, for that is all I have as every last herb for miles about is covered with deep snow. Still, he would be a comfort.

I have barely the strength to keep a fire burning and food and water in my belly. Strange thoughts and conversations drift thru my mind. I forbear when the glutton scratches at my door, for my ears still ring. I have done many a fool thing in my life, but shooting at him is among the most foolish. When I ask myself how I could have pulled the trigger of a buffalo gun indoors, I can think only of the man who is said to have taken off his clothes and jumped naked into a briar patch and when asked why replied because it seemed to be the thing to do at the time. Humor is a weak stick to wield against such a formidable foe as the infection in my hand, but I must keep my spirits up, for dire circumstances are only worsened by a glum face.

I dreamed some other time that a strange person walked thru my door and gave me a draught of laudanum, and then I had the best sleep I can remember for a week. It is a wonder how powerful a dream can be. I have tried to dream it again but cannot.

I am thinking about David's tale of the Scapeweed Goat and his Ewe and about the great contrast between them and K and me. The story is terrible and haunts me. K and I seldom spoke in words about our love, for she was modest. She was not overly shy when it came to such matters tho, and was ever willing to make our bed a pleasurable place with tender endearments and some little laughter or tickling or other sweet foolishness that is natural between a man and a woman when they fit well together. I have never understood why a man would pay money to watch displays of public lewdness or how a woman could permit herself to be so used and smile all the while, for I have seen them outside their bordellos in San Francisco and other cities. It is a great sadness to me that people should act in this way, and I ofttimes wonder if they have drunk of 'scapeweed.

As I think on it, I would gladly drink it myself at this juncture, for the pain in my hand is so great that sometimes I would do anything to make it go away. I have known pain before but disregarded it for I always knew it would pass, save for bruises on bones or ribs, which are excruciating and seem to last forever. The list of what I have to help me is short.

1. Salt and plenty of it.

2. Whiskey, tho only a few cups and that not to drink but to pour on me, which burns like fire.

3. Axle grease, which I dare not use in such deep wounds, for it is better that they get the air.

4. Mustard for plasters and blistering, which my hand does not need for it is hot enough to blister of its own accord.

5. Horse meat, but that will only draw a bruise and it is bad doctoring to put rotting flesh on top of rotting.

6. Gunpowder, but the wounds are too deep to burn out.

7. The herb of dreams, but only three pipes full remain and I must hoard them should I have to remove the hand, which would be impossible without some help.

The herb of dreams is a mixed blessing, for the oblivion it

confers is ofttimes marred by disquieting dreams and notions. Two days ago, or so I reckon tho it may be three, I was forced to lance my hand for it was stopped up unlike my wrist which is open and drains well, and my forearm which is healing. It had got filled with pus and was hot and swollen to the bursting point, and gave me constant pain so I could scarce do my chores or think or sleep or hold food on my stomach.

I jumped off a cliff into a river once when my life was in danger from Indians. The fall was exhilarating, and in those three or four seconds before I hit I knew that all would be well if I lived and if I died I would not feel it long. But to pierce my own hand with a sharp knife was a far different matter, for the piercing would be neither my end nor immediate salvation, but bring only pain. There was naught else to do tho, so I began my preparations. I boiled water and made a bucket of salt wash. I set aside a rag to catch the putrescence. I cut strips of latex from my slicker to use as drains and in one end of each fashioned a knot and in the other cut a slit. I bent my bucket bail in half and put a small hook in each end and boiled this instrument and the latex and my thin knife and laid them on my table. All the while Andrew watched me from the safety of his biscuit tin but did not speak, for tho he had come out of hiding he still somewhat feared me after the shot I took at the glutton. When all was prepared I settled my pillows in my big chair and packed my pipe with the herb of dreams. When I had smoked half of it and could feel its effects beginning on me, I reached out and took up my knife and plunged it thru the holes in my hand and out the other side and screamed in pain and fell back on my pillows in a swoon.

No man who has lived on the frontier or seen the effects of war can too easily be overcome by odors. I have lived among men who have not washed for three months when there was no water for that. I once descended into a small valley where I saw some Indian teepees and when I neared was assailed by the stench, for the army had massacred the hapless inhabitants and left them to rot. I never believed myself to be immortal and have not worried overly much about my passing, but such an odor carries with it a presentiment of doom and so invests that natural conclusion of life with horror, and strong tho a man may be he may weaken when the stench of putrefaction emanates from his own self.

What came next I remember the way a man sees across a hot desert floor where everything is distorted by heat, for my task was only half done. Before I could make myself sick by thinking on it, I plunged the doubled over bail thru the holes in my hand, and hooked the pieces of latex to it and drew them thru my palm and out the back, and put sticks thru the slits I had made in the latex so they should not slip out, and plunged my hand into the salt wash. After I had cleaned and dried it, I forced myself to finish my pipe before I poured whiskey on my hand, and then once again fell back in a swoon, and if I dreamed I do not remember what.

My fire was down when I came to my senses, so I built it up and made myself eat and drink, and passed that day in a delirium. I remember talking to my wife, who bathed my hand and comforted me and soothed my brow. Next to her sat my son, who was a comely youth of ten tho I do not know how he aged so little unless time where he is be slowed. Another moment he talked to me thru Andrew's mouth. Another time the glutton came to me and would have torn me asunder save some force held him back tho he was close enough that I could feel his stinking breath on my face. Yet another time I conversed with David's great-grandfather Ralph, who entreated me to watch over and protect David, and I saw the Scapeweed Goat and his Ewe in their slow, macabre dance of death, and many other marvels and horrors I cannot remember now.

That was not a day I wish to remember tho I never will forget it. None the less my fever was much abated and my hand drained and greatly improved by my crude surgery, and I have learned again that a man may do things he thought impossible when the need is on him, and confess some modest pride in my accomplishment tho I know too well that pride may precede a fall.

February 16

A blizzard today, so bad a man cannot see his hand at arm's length, which in my case could be a blessing. I am glad poor Duke is dead. He should certainly starve under these conditions were he not, for I could not tend to him. Better the swift mercy of a bullet than the slow and groveling weakness of starvation. I cannot stand to see any animal die that way, or man either, for I have seen Indians who have come to that pass and it is a pitiable end for people of a proud race.

My hand continues to drain. It is not so swollen nor does it hurt much. Withal I have a sinking feeling in my gut for I see some darkening in my fingers, which is a bad sign, so I will write more while I may.

There are times when it is better to lose a fight than win one. K's mother and father had fought a bitter campaign to prevent me from taking her to the wilderness and I had fought back. K herself was fearful of what might happen to our child, but I painted a rosy picture with my glib tongue and off we went. And then less than six months later their fears were borne out and my rosy picture had turned into the tortured scrawl of a madman given charcoal and paper and told to draw a portrait of the devils that plague him.

My son was dead and buried in a crude grave. My wife, not yet turned eighteen years of age, lay on what I feared was her death bed. Her long blond hair that had shone in the sun like gold had lost its luster and lay like old, limp straw upon her pillow. Her eyes were lined with dark circles and, once as bright and sparkling blue as the surface of a pond on a sunlit day, had grown empty, dull, and gray, that same pond when low clouds hide the sun and the rain has yet to fall and clear the air. Her cheeks, once full and tinted like young peaches, were pale and wan and sunken. Her lips, once as fresh and wholesome as ripe cherries, were of a purple hue, and thin and drawn. Her breasts, once firm and pert and proud, lay flaccid on her chest, their darker parts flat and diminished. Her whole body, once so strong and shapely, so full of life and vigor, was weak and wasted, no more substantive than a shadow cast by moonlight. And I was the agent of this mayhem, for I had brought her there and placed her at the mercy of the Guards and in the path of the little tiny bee that stings, the Wasp of Death.

What a miraculous instrument is a man's mind! I can close my eyes and I am there. The starlight is faint and the sound of night birds and insects muted. Our mare and gelding are but dark shapes as they munch on their grass. My ears are ringing and my stomach is grumbling and my heart is beating wildly. My thoughts and emotions fly like buckshot, and I am assailed by love and hatred and fear and anger.

To this day, I can pray the prayers I prayed then, and word for word. "Oh dear Jesus," I prayed, "I will give Thee my life if Thou wilt spare that of my darling K."

I invoked the name of His father, tho mine had told me it was wrong to bargain with the Lord, for His ways were mysterious and a man could only take what was given him whether it be of riches or of poverty, whether of bliss or of woe.

"Dear Father in Heaven," I prayed, "give me my wife's life and I will give Thee mine and praise Thy name for all eternity."

And so the Great Bear swung in his circle and our fire died to embers. And so my feet turned numb while my wife stirred and slept and stirred again. And so I held her tiny hand in mine that my strength might flow into her, and so at last when the stars in the east were fading did I sleep with my chin on my chest and dream that she called my name and squeezed my hand and told me that she loved me to eternity and then sighed and slipped away from me.

The next I knew, David's hand was on my shoulder and the sun was in the sky. Only half awake, I smiled down at my wife who had turned her head to smile at me.

David gazed at her, then over his shoulder to the trees on the far side of our valley. "Thou slept."

"A moment or two," said I, and laid her hand on her bed and stretched and yawned. "What do you see?"

"Nothing. Rather sense and feel in my bones." Swiftly he turned and kneeled in his grease soaked clothes by K's bed. "I am sorry, J. I could not have helped had I been at her side."

His words made no sense to me. "What?"

For answer, he reached to her and with his two fingers closed her eyes.

"What?" said I, in sudden daze. "What?"

"It is a peaceful death. Thou seest that she hath a smile upon her lips."

I could not understand. For all my fears that she should die and all my prayers that she should live, I could not understand. "What?" said I, the only word I knew, and stood and almost fell, my feet were so numbed. "What?"

"Sit ere thou fallest," said he in a harsh tone. "And give me that cup."

I obeyed like a child and, astonished, watched and laughed when he lifted her head and held the cup to her lips, for it seemed a thing of great humor to give a dead woman water to drink. "What? What?" said I, and wiped the tears from my cheeks where they were running down.

David waved his hand over her in a manner strange to me, then threw away the water and inexplicably kissed his closed fist in the circle made by his thumb and forefinger before turning on me. "Calm thyself, I adjure thee, for I yet may hope to save thy life."

The knowledge of her death swept thru me like the howl of wolves thru winter woods, and I was left chilled to my bones and shaking with anger. "Give me the cup, damn you! Take your hand away from her!"

He did as I commanded, and stood and looked down at me with the full authority of an Adept talking to a peasant. "Wouldst live, J?"

Emotions passed through me as quickly as sticks are swept over a waterfall one after the other, and so my anger passed and was replaced by a listlessness that weighed so heavy on my head I could not hold it up. "No. She is gone then? No. I care not."

"The Guards are here. They are watching us."

"Good. Let them feast their eyes."

"And when they have eaten their fill, kill thee."

"I care not, I tell you."

"Not even to avenge her death?"

"To what end, damn us both? Will it bring her back to life? You avenge her. I care not."

"Thou spake different yesterday."

"She was alive yesterday."

"And thou art still alive today."

"Go away, David. I will lay her next to my son and mourn her, and they may slay me if they wish."

So saying, I turned to her, but as I bent to lift her, David plucked my revolver from my waistband and held it to my head as he leaned over next to me. "Give me this one little minute to explain myself," said he in my ear, "and then thou mayst decide for thyself."

I hesitated, but was not to be deterred. "Give me this one little minute to count to three," said I patiently, "and then kill you or die trying if you do not let me go."

"Thou wilt not get so far as half the way to her grave before they cut you down. Hast not listened to me? That they remove the heads of dead Wanderers and return them to Home to prove their deaths?"

"We are not Wanderers."

"But I am and thou hast succored me! They will fear what I may have told thee, and will have thy head and that of thy wife."

She lay but a foot below my face, and I remembered his words of the night before, that Wanderers who were caught suffered death by a terrible smoke and that the heads of others were brought back as proof their flight had been stayed, and my heart sank as I pictured her poor mutilated flesh, and my gorge rose and great sobs tore from my chest and my tears spilled on her gown. "What would you have me do, then?" I at last found the strength and breath to ask.

David patted my shoulder and placed my revolver in my hand. "We must carry her from her shelter into thy cabin."

Somewhat in control of myself, I holstered my revolver and stood erect to gaze at the woods beyond us. "But why?"

"Even now they circle and will come at us in threes within the hour if we remain outside, for they fear no man in the open. But if we are inside they will fear thee because they cannot see thy gun, for the Weaving Dance can be done only when the weapon is in sight. Then three will come from the south and hidden by her shelter take her away to draw you out so they may attack. If she be in with us they will keep their distance and come at night when our traps might work and we will have them somewhat at our mercy."

Her head cut off, and her body left to lie and be picked apart by the carrion eaters, the foxes and the birds and the feral pigs that roamed those parts! Mine too, tho I did not care so much for I deserved no less, but could not preserve her were I dead too. Resolved, I steeled myself to the task. "Very well," said I, and turned to lift her.

We made a sad and unlikely procession as I see us now. I

carried K, and David, in his greasy clothes, walked behind me with her pallet so we need not lay her on the hard dirt floor. When we had her laid down, we ran back out, David to dismantle her shelter so it might not impede our view, I to gather our food and water and knives. When we returned I washed my wife and covered her and lay down next to her for the last time, and fell into a deep slumber.

The sun was started down the western sky when I waked. At first I thought David had fled and left me alone, but then discovered him on the porch when I went out to relieve myself.

"Thou hast slept well."

"To my shame," said I, and gazed about our valley. The scene was peaceful. Our crops lay green in the sun with the rich brown earth peeking thru. A gentle breeze from the south stirred the trees, and the only sound was a distant crow. "Well?" I asked.

"Three there," said he, pointing to the east, "and three there."

I could not see them, so went in to our trunk to fetch the glass K's father had given us. "Where?"

He pointed. "Directly below the large tree that stands on the horizon, and to the side of the willows in the shade."

I picked out the first three easily, two asleep and one standing and watching in our direction, then the second three next to the willows. "Six, then," said I.

"Nay. Behind thy cabin under the great tree thou callest a hickory."

I went in and stepped around the wagon bed we had stood up for a barrier. There thru the hole in the chinking we had cut in the back wall the day before, I saw the last three and knew we were surrounded.

There was little else to do. I got some corn bread and a cup of water and joined David on the porch to eat.

"Hast seen them?" said he.

"They are there."

"Keep watch, then," said he, and turned to go inside. "Wake me when the sun touches the hills."

"That I will. And David," said I, and spit out some water.

"Aye?"

"I am determined to live thru this."

"Aye," said he, and nodded.

Tho I think he knew my thought, I told him anyway. "And when we are done with them, I will kill you. For I owe my wife and son no less, and deserve that pleasure."

February 19

I am neither the first nor the last man in this world to lose a wife and child, but I felt I was, as must every man. Happily I am no longer angry or even saddened, save rarely, for it is true that time erases pain, and fifty-five years of wanderings and adventures is a long time. The sadness and pain increased when I lay with other women, for I ever compared them to my beautiful K, who chose me over three wealthier and better educated rivals and loved me to the exclusion of other men. Always too I wondered what our life might have been like were we not cut off unnaturally from each other by that little tiny stinging bee, and held to her memory as a man caught in a desert clings to his canteen tho it hold but a thimble full of water.

My greatest regret and sadness tho is that I never had a child of my own to love. I loved the one we had so briefly as much as any man can, but that is not the same as being greeted at the door by a smiling face, or hearing footsteps running from a monstrous dream in the night, or feeling a tiny hand

wrapped trustingly around a finger. It is not the same as guid-
ing a son or daughter into manhood or womanhood, or having
grandchildren to pamper and prattle on about incessantly. I
admit I am sentimental, and tho I know there be many who
have learned to despise their offspring, I would have held mine
close to me and cherished them forever.

I was by no means so philosophical that long ago day. With
vengeance on my mind I kept watch on the waiting Guards
that afternoon much as, for the past three days, I have kept
watch on my fingers and the blackness that creeps down them,
and with the same trepidation. The comparison is not exact
for my fingers have no mind of their own and the blackness is
but an effect of a disease, but in either case they would take
my life without any compunction, and my fate lies in my ability
to remove the menace. I will say tho that it was far easier to
contemplate killing nine men than it is to envision cutting off
five of my own fingers, especially when I am already missing
one on the other hand, and have none to spare.

Our plan supposed they would attack after dark, and depended in part on their believing that both David and I should
remain in the cabin. So we prepared ourselves, David by arm-
ing himself with two knives and a bag full of the Wasps of
Death that we had taken from the Guards who had previously
attacked us and slathering pork grease on his exposed parts, I
by gathering wads of cotton to put in my ears. When the time
came, David got his head out the hole we had dug under the
west side of the cabin where there were no Guards, and I
watched thru my glass that I had hung in the doorway and
trained my rifle as close as possible at the three Guards by the
willows. Presently I heard the whistle of a bird and David
thumping his foot against the floor, which was his signal to tell
me the bird that whistled had no feathers. Immediately I took
a deep breath and fired, reloaded and fired again, and then
took my glass and gun and retired behind the wagon bed. A
second later when I touched the spot where the hole was, I

discovered David was gone and said a silent prayer that he should reach the barrel I kept as a cover over our spring without being discovered.

A seventy-five year old man forgets what it is like to be twenty years old. He forgets how it feels to be lean and lithe and strong, to take joy in the work and movement of his muscles and limbs, and to thrill in heavy labor and danger. A twenty year old youngster revels in his body but looks on his strength and agility as his due, and when a task is at hand lights into it with a verve, the more so when he has a cause.

My wife and son lay dead. Their executioners waited without my door, and I thirsted for their blood. Every nerve and muscle and bone in my body, even to every hair on my head, beckoned them to their deaths. Sweat poured out of me and ran down my torso, for I would not avenge my wife and son wearing clothes soaked in pig fat. My revolver was loaded, my two spare cylinders full in a small open pouch I had hung on my belt. My knives, the broad and the slim, were sharp as the razor I shaved with, and loose in their sheaths.

My memory of the battle with the Guards consists of a series of vivid flashes, like a night lit by lightning. I had no sense of time, for its normal course was suspended and broken into pieces. I remember waiting in a silence so complete it nullified bird and insect and frog sounds, for I was not listening for them save only if they ceased, which should be a sign. I remember a surge of elation when I heard our first trap spring, and imagined one of David's upside down catapults driving its pointed stakes into the back of a crawling Guard, and counted one as down.

I remember too hearing a tin cup in which we had put some pebbles fall to the ground, and knew that the Guards to my rear were close enough to David for him to surprise them with bees of their own manufacture and in other ways occupy their attention. I chanced a quick look out my rear spy hole and saw in the dim light the silhouette of a figure with a spear sticking out of its chest rise and stagger a few steps and fall before my attention was diverted by the sound of another jangling cup.

A man lay or stood against the east side of my cabin. Quiet as Andrew asleep, I padded to the slanted spy hole we had dug thru the chinking on that side and looked into the mirror we had placed there just in time to see a second join his fellow, and the pair gesticulate one to the front and one to the rear. Before they had a chance to move tho, I reached out with my broad knife and slashed thru the cords holding the log we had suspended under the eaves, and had the satisfaction of seeing them both crushed when it fell on them.

Three, as I guessed, left in the front then, and two in the rear. My cotton in my ears, for I no longer needed to hear, I moved to the slit cut thru the wagon bed, thru which I could see my front door, which looked bright as day compared to the utter darkness inside. What seemed scant seconds later, tho it may have been minutes, I saw the light occluded by a shape and heard a quick drumming hail I took to be the sound of Wasps of Death striking my wagon bed. Without a thought I slashed the cord that restrained another bent sapling and had but a fleeting second to enjoy seeing it catch one shape across the chest before I was busy firing at the other two who came in low.

The cotton helped but little, which was why I knew better than to fire at the glutton from inside my cabin here, for the sound was awesome and could be felt in the gut and bones as well as in the ears, tho not great enough to obliterate the screams that tore from the throat of one of the Guards. My last shot I used against the first Guard, who was caught upright in the doorway by the stake piercing his chest, which was the last of his worries in this world, for he was thrown off the spear and out the door with his heart destroyed by a slug of lead.

One in the ditch I had dug to drain my potato patch, for it was low and collected water. Two beside my wall, for three.

Three more in my doorway, for six. At least one got by David, for seven. And two more whose whereabouts I could not tell.

What went before was a simple matter compared with the wait that followed, it being no easy task to wait for whatever a man knows not. Once, in my state and thinking I saw one in the doorway move, I fired into him, but was rewarded by naught more than silence. I feared leaving my watch over the corpses on my floor and feared not leaving them to look out my rearward spy hole. At long last I heard a low whistle outside my door, bade David to enter, and watched as he snaked thru, around the wagon bed, and collapsed at my side.

"Well?" I asked.

"Two of mine slain," said he in a labored voice. "One remains free and I ken not where he be."

"Eight then," said I, and drew away in alarm, for I had felt the slickness of blood on his arm. "You are cut!"

"Aye. In three places, for he was an old one and wily, and came upon me from the rear. And thou?"

"Whole," said I. "Not so much as one little nick or scratch."

"Thy boots are on thy feet?"

"No."

"Pull them on then, lest thou steppest on one of the bees lying about on the floor."

I did as he ordered, and wished I could do something to help him, but he told me he was beyond help for the greased clothes were of little value against such great cuts, and bade me give him some water, which I did.

"What do I do now?" I asked.

"Wait for the light of day as he will," said he. "Then thou must venture out and meet him and face the Weaving Dance and a swarm of bees, for there is no other way. But thou must do so alone, for I will not be here to help thee, so pay close attention that thou mayst prevail."

And then he bade me repeat my lesson of the night before

when he had explained to me the Weaving Dance. He listened as I repeated that I must keep my eyes on my assailant's belly, shoot from my waist, and aim by pointing at him naturally by my instinct alone.

"And how will he come?" he asked.

"From side to side and twisting, and I must fire two or three times calmly but quickly once I anticipate his direction, for single shots are simple to avoid."

"Do all this and thou wilt make the number nine and be done with them," said he. "And then bury thy wife and me too if thou wilt and quit these parts, for thy wife and son will be avenged enough."

"And if I do not, but seek out the others?"

"Why, then they will slay thee, which would be a waste, for one of you should survive. Hast more water?"

I held the jug while he drank, then set it aside and sat next to him with my back against the wagon bed. "One should survive," I repeated in a musing way. "You are right, David. Survive to testify, and send an army to destroy this aberration."

"No, friend J. No!" His hand found mine in the darkness and gripped it. "To survive as a victory o'er them, for I think there has never been one and the time is due. But I beg thee tell no man. Let the peasants and Civilizers rise up and destroy Home themselves as they will ere long. I would not have us inspected and our history bandied about to make my people a laughing stock, for our purpose was as noble as our name, tho our end fell short of the goal."

"And the slaughter of the innocents in the meantime?"

"They are all innocent," said he in a sad tone, "and all culpable."

"Yet some might still be saved," I persisted. "Your son, for one."

"My son?" David asked with a sad chuckle. "My son? Oh, J! There is so much more thou dost not know. But I will make a barter with thee. If thou promiseth not to tell the world of the Noble Savages, and let their remnants scatter on the winds and sink into oblivion, I will finish my tale and tell thee of my culpability. Wilt promise? And listen?"

February 26

I had feared I would not live to write these pages. I had proposed next to set down the end of David's tale and the resolution of the fight with the one remaining Guard, but the events of the past week have been so extraordinary that I must write them out first in order to clarify them for myself lest I get them so muddled in my brain that I cannot tell the difference between dream and reality.

I have cut off my hand two inches above my wrist.

It is a frightening thing to watch your fingers turn black, to see the blackness creep down them toward your hand, and to know you cannot stop it.

I slept but little the night when I last wrote and that poorly from the glutton outside my door and the wind howling like a thousand ghosts from the past and the worry about my hand stirring about in my head like a poisonous brew concocted by some evil, lurking Preeminent One I could neither see nor hear. The next day between my chores, which I stretched to keep my mind occupied, I sat and stared at my fingers and tried to ignore Andrew's carping denunciations of his provender, which was I think but his own worry for me disguised, for he also chided me at length for not chewing thru my arm as mice do when a foot may be mangled.

I have read about men they call yogis or yogas, I forget

which. It is said they can overpower their bodies by exercises of the mind, which is a wondrous facility, but I have not the learning of how it is done any more than I have the faith of a mustard seed, tho I tried by staring at my fingers and telling the blackness to recede. I thought on it when I went to sleep that night, but when I woke in the morning the blackness was into my hand and I knew that time was short, for it was proceeding ever faster. My hand was dying and rotting off and would take me with it.

Rarely have I known such anger. Better the glutton had slain me than I her. Better I had been carried off by the pox or been buried by an avalanche or frozen to death. Better that day I jumped off the cliff I had landed on the rocks and come to a quick end. Out of my anger came another plan, for I was not willing to go without taking the male with me. Accordingly I spent half the day lying on my bearskin on the floor in front of my door busily drilling a hole thru the wood large enough to fit the muzzle of my rifle thru. I then hacked grooves in some firewood to serve as a stand to support the stock. That night before I went to bed I stuck my rifle thru the hole and covered the muzzle with a chunk of horse meat, then closed the door, tied down the rifle, set it on cock, and ran a thong from the trigger to my bed where I could find it readily. That done, I stuffed cotton waste in my ears and lay down to sleep with Andrew by my head on the pillow to keep me company.

That was the night of my visions, which was strange because I had smoked none of the herb of dreams. I once read in a newspaper a tale called A Christmas Carol by Chas. Dickens, another Englishman. In this tale three spirits visited E. Scrooge, who was a miserly man. I have not been miserly, but also received three spirits, each as powerful as those in Mr. Dickens's tale, and a horde of others too who populated my dreams and moaned and rolled their eyes and would no doubt have clanked their chains had they any.

I might have been the Scapeweed Goat awaiting his death

in the amphitheater, for I was confronted with a sea of faces. Many were blank as I turned to regard them, but some detached themselves from the general mass and floated toward me, moving slowly at first as they approached to hurl at me the carrots and onions and pigs' heads of my past, then faster as they whisked over my head and disappeared behind me, some silently, some hissing accusations or hooting derisively, tho I remember not their order for the most part nor the words of any of them.

Thus came K's mother and father, who chased me down a muddy street and slipped and fell and cursed my name, but I kept the horse I was riding to a steady pace for I could not look them in the eye after telling them of her death, and my own mother too, on whom I turned my back in spite of her entreaties to stay, for I would not live in those parts.

Thus too came the men I had killed at my gold mine, rattling their bones at me and howling that they awaited me at the bottom of the shaft all covered over with tailings, and a gambler whom I shot under a table in Sacramento, and a horse I had ridden to death one night in anger after I had drunk too much whiskey, and two swans and a cygnet I slew one afternoon when I was assailed by self pity and eaten with bitter hatred of all things beautiful.

Thus too came an old farmer outside Cleveland who smoked a pipe and took my labor of building him a fence but denied me my bread in recompense, and a young woman in Georgia who smiled and licked her lips at me but turned cold when her husband rode up on his horse, and a dead child in Mississippi whose portrait I painted and whose mother swooned when she beheld it.

Thus too came a harridan in St. Louis who drove me out of her boarding house because her dog would come and sit by me instead of her, and a storekeeper in Boston from whom I stole a loaf of bread and a piece of cheese when I was hungry, and an ancient hag in Pottstown who accused me of stealing her garden spade tho I had never seen her before and stood before her with naught but my brushes and paints and the clothes on my back.

Thus too came the faces of a thousand portraits small and large that I had painted to be secreted in brooches or hung openly on walls, faces who damned me for flattering them too much or not enough.

And more, a succession of men and women and children I had seen in my life. Ranks of soldiers with bare feet and gaunt faces and scurvy, but guns in working order. Children with stringy hair and dark eyes as empty as their bellies. Red men dispossessed and yellow men worked to skin and bone and a Negro in Alabama I saw lynched but dared not help tho he had done no wrong, for I feared the crazed mob and fled even as they set torches to his poor maimed feet. Women old before their time and tired beyond weeping. Faceless and sexless and ageless husks of people, their souls sucked out of them in mines and fields and factories, until I cried out in pain and cowered and hid my head and spun about slowly to a low thrumming sound that rose in pitch while I spun faster and faster, until the sound was a high shriek that pierced my ears and there was silence all about me.

How long I lay there I know not, but when I came to my senses I was floating thru the air and came to firm ground on a high promontory. Below me I could see the world as thru a glass or an eagle's eye, and the people were all small as ants crawling about and running this way and that to no purpose and carrying great loads to no destination. There was beauty from that vantage point that I beheld as if thru a stereopticon, but whether I was plucked from hither to yon or the scenes were changed in front of me by some unseen hand I do not know.

Now I was in a steep valley where a high waterfall plunging from above dissolved into rainbows, now on a precipice looking over a vast canyon that was filled with a marvel of shadow and light. Now I was viewing the bold reds and yellows of autumn in the northern mountains, now on a hummock in a limitless swamp over whose cypress spiked horizon lay a fat glowing moon that turned the night orange and dropped heavy shadows at my feet, and I could smell smoke and hear the booming call of ancient beasts and the whine of musquitoes. Now I was on a flat plain with the pierced bowl of heaven a twinkling black dome over my head, now on a levee with mist rising to reveal a great river.

The scenes changed so fast that I was given but a glimpse of each. A tree fat with red leaves, a twisted vine covered with magenta blossoms, a waterspout curling grayly upward from a bay. There stood a dun stallion against pewter clouds, there hung a cardinal like a flame in the air. There a daffodil poked thru the snow, and there an icicle hung from an eave and gave the morning diamonds. There was a thin green snake coiled in the sun, there a bursting milkweed pod. There was a dainty, stolid ladybug, and there a drop of dew hung like a jewel on a spider's web, and there the eye of a honeybee and the spiked leg of a grasshopper and many more wonders too numerous to recollect or recount.

I sat, then fell to one side and lay in a curled ball, wept like a child, and fell asleep. When I woke I was standing again on that same high promontory, which had become bathed in a white light. And there were flowers such as I had never seen growing all about me, and some paces to my side three figures whose feet were hidden by the flowers.

"What are you doing here?" asked the first, who was my wife but would not let me approach her.

I did not know and said as much.

"Then thou must leave, for it be not yet thy time," said the next, who I knew by his voice as David tho I could not see his face clearly.

How I cannot tell, but I knew also that he would brook no argument, so turned to leave tho my heart was heavy.

"The snow," said the third in the voice of a child.

I turned to see my son's face, which was quickly hid by the light.

"Yes," said they all together to me. "The snow is thy medicine. We will wait for thee."

And I felt small warm lips brush my face and woke to darkness and the sound of the glutton outside my door, and tho I reached for my thong and held it in my hand, did not pull on it, for my dream was still with me and I saw that the glutton had no animosity toward me but was only like every other creature in the world who wanted no more than to eat and live. And so I could not take the life I had desired but hours before, and let him eat my meat for there is none other to be had in the valley.

February 27

The Bible teaches that if a man's hand offend him he should cut it off and cast it from him. I have read that this may be called an allegory, whereby a lesson is taught by things that have other meanings. I have not held a Bible in my hands for over fifty years, but this teaching that does not apply to me comes readily to mind, for I cut off my hand and cast it from me even if it did me no offense. Rather it protected me and served to offend a glutton that was trying to harm me, and I do not recall any mention of gluttons in the Bible.

I have seen arms cut off, and legs too. When I was a young man the patient drank whiskey until he was drunk, after which three or four men held him down while a surgeon or other experienced practitioner went about his business. Later the task was made easier by ether, which is a wondrous drug. Once I myself took charge of that onerous task when there was no surgeon about, and because I had no ether poured whiskey into my patient until he was senseless.

I had neither ether nor whiskey enough nor tools nor any help, and tho I am not the first man in the history of the world to cut off his own hand, I do not recommend the procedure for any but the most stout of heart and am glad it was my hand and not my foot, for I doubt if I could have got thru my leg bone with a single stroke of an ax.

I wish I had named my son before I buried him so I could have called him by name when I saw him and he spoke to me and gave me the gift of snow, which I was blessed with in excess but had been too blind to see as an agent that I might put to good use. Sometimes the simplest things evade a man because they are so obvious. Obvious or arcane, I learned again how a curse may become a blessing, for the snow that prevented the flies that could have given me maggots and saved me the trouble of cutting off my hand became my best ally and saved me the trouble of dying. This is how I did it, and tho my preparations took the whole morning they were fast enough, for I had become modestly proficient with one hand.

Again, I melted snow and boiled the water 'til my cabin was filled with steam. I cooked a pot of stew made of horse meat sweetened with bear fat to which I added salt and two hands full of grain, enough to last me three days, and opened the rest of my stores for Andrew in case the time my three spirits talked about should be brief, for I knew not whether to expect minutes or days or years. I shortened the handle on my heavy ax so it would not be unwieldy, and sharpened and honed it and my knives as a barber would his razors. I prepared a tourniquet and fixed it loosely about my arm above my elbow. I strung my needle with a length of stout thread. I placed my broad farrier's buttress in the coals to heat for cauterizing. I drew the outline of a wide flap or tongue of skin on my forearm

with the same ink I am now using. I filled my pipe with the
herb of dreams. And last, when all else was ready, I brought
inside some buckets of snow that I dumped in an empty keg
that I laid on its side on my table, then made myself comfortable in my big chair, lit my pipe, and plunged my hand and
forearm to the elbow into the snow.

Ether may be the best medicine and whiskey a close second,
but cold in my circumstances out distances both, for a man
may not cut off his own hand when he is sleeping or drunk.
When the cold became painful I drew out my arm part way
and tested it with my knife. This I did twice more before the
skin was numb. When it was, I stroked Andrew's head once
and went to the flat block I keep by the fire for cutting meat
and sat cross legged before it and shook the buzzing from my
head and went to work.

First I tightened my tourniquet. Then I cut along the line I
had drawn, which hurt no more than pulling a deep sliver,
peeled back the skin, and with a rag soaked in salt water tied
back the flap to keep it out of my way. Very fast then, before I
could reflect overly much on what I was doing, I took up my
ax and aimed just below the inside edge of the skin flap and
struck my arm with all my might.

I have seen men shot and walking around as normal as on a
Sunday stroll for two or three minutes before the pain arrests
them, and so it was when I struck off my arm, for cold may
numb flesh but does not touch bone. My ax cut clean thru and
stuck in the block. Praying that I would not swoon before I was
done, I pulled the farrier's buttress from the fire and clapped it
to my stump to sear it and dropped the tongue of skin over
the open wound but could get only one stitch in before giving
up because the needle would not easily go thru the skin which
slipped about and rubbed over the end of my bones, so tied it
down with soaked rags because I was beginning to hurt.

I have bled worse from a cut on my finger and do not think
I lost so much as a cup of blood and much of that from seepage

when I loosed my tourniquet, for the cold had constricted my vessels. There was little time to think on that tho, for my stomach was queasy, my forehead had broken out in a cold sweat, and I was growing faint, so I moved to my chair and plunged my stump into the keg of snow. There, with my task completed, I sucked on my pipe while my bandages chilled, then lay my arm in my sling, placed Andrew on my shoulder to get the comfort of his voice in my ear, and let myself fall into a deep faint.

That was five days ago. When I woke I was somewhat surprised but more than pleased to find I could walk to build up my fire, which had died down to coals. While I waited for the kindling to catch I drank some water, and while I was at it chanced to see my hand, but kept the water down altho with some effort.

There are better things for a man to see than his own hand lying on a chopping block, comfort tho I took in the knowledge that it could not kill me there. Steeling myself, I wrapped it in a rag and stored it with the part of Duke I had in the cubbyhole behind my cabin so I might bury it later when the ground thawed, for tho I still felt no animosity toward the glutton I was not so enamored of him that I wished to feed him my hand.

Soon my fire was brisk and my stew bubbling. My stomach did not want any, but I ate some spoons full. That done and my stores closed up again, for it appeared I would live a little longer after all, I checked my stump and found the color good and the bleeding but an ooze, so took Andrew with me and lay down to sleep.

The next day I did nothing but eat and sleep and talk to Andrew. It was a pleasant enough way to spend a day until he grew contentious and would not agree that chopping off an arm was easier than chomping one off. At last, too irritated with his arguments to listen any longer, I agreed that I was not mouse enough to chew off my own arm and shut him in his biscuit tin and drank half of my remaining whiskey, and slept before a roaring fire.

March 1

My left hand has ached fearsomely since the middle of last night, almost as if it were still there. I have heard men complain of feelings in missing limbs but, because the little finger of my right hand never ached in the many years since it was lopped off, always thought they were daft. Now I see I was wrong. I look at the spot where my hand should be and see nothing, but feel its presence. This mysterious ache is sometimes said to presage a change in the weather. I hope that is the case here, for I should welcome clear skies and a melt.

But to return to David, for I wish to complete his story between times I busy myself making up my pack to escape this prison valley the minute conditions allow, lest nature turn on me with a fresh onslaught of snow.

My cabin was so dark I could not see my hand held before my nose. The night was warm and muggy, and the odors of the dead Guards on my floor and of David's clothes soaked in rancid pig fat assailed my nostrils. Of sound I could hear none save my own and David's breathing, and from the outside the usual chorus of frogs and insects. As much as I have been trapped here this winter, I was more so that night and dared not for my life stir beyond our cramped fort.

"Hast received of a sudden what thou wished for, but not been satisfied?" David asked after a long silence.

So unexpected was his voice that I started and my heart raced. "What?" I asked in return, not immediately grasping his meaning.

"Three summers past, one small field of wheat in the far south of the valley grew to maturity. Hearing of this, the authorities confiscated every last grain and that autumn apportioned them out to certain peasants for planting. When the snow melted in the spring the new wheat looked healthy, and as the summer passed the rust was seen to be abated and golden fields of wheat once again waved under the sun, and smiles returned to the faces of the Noble Savages and laughter and gaiety spread through the valley."

"And so their prayers were answered," said I, tho I cared not overly much under the present circumstances. "And so much the better for everyone."

The Noble Savages agreed, and with enough wheat for seed and for bread on the table, tho not in abundance, they believed they had discovered the key to the Infinitude's pleasure and rejoiced with dancing and singing and prayers of thanksgiving. That harvest moon the Feast of the Gesture of Propitiation was louder and more boisterous than ever, and when a powerful aphrodisiac was administered in place of the Potion of Expiation to the sacrificial pair, the people cheered as the two unfortunate souls rutted for the last time in their lives, and they ran forward in high humor to hurl their offerings and kill the Scapeweed Goat and his Ewe, and spent the remainder of the night in raucous celebration.

The Noble Savages' problems seemed to be solved, and so they might have been had it not been for a perverse streak that inhabits mankind of whatever stripe or lineage. It is said that the Devil makes mischief for idle hands. Whether or not there is a Devil the principle holds true, for a rumor was born in the midst of plenty that, like the green blades of wheat lying dormant under the snow, gained strength thru the idle season.

No one knew whence came the rumor, but it involved a

pouch of wheat a Trader had supposedly got from Civilization and given to his brother, who was the peasant whose field had been the first to bear grain in five years. The Trader and the peasant denied this allegation, for they did not wish to suffer the Smoke of Retribution, but the rumor persisted tho the Preeminent One deemed it heretical and stated publicly with irrefutable proofs that the Infinitude alone was responsible for the revival of the wheat.

Many believed the Preeminent One as a matter of course, but there were others for whom a pronouncement from on high did not suffice. Small in number, they included many of Home's prominent citizens who, during the enforced idleness of the winter, had talked among themselves and renewed and strengthened the cult of the Civilizers by asking questions that no one, the Preeminent One least of all, wished to answer. Why, they asked, had the authorities refused to import seed grain in the first place and, once they had, why would they not admit that it had come from Civilization? Why had the Noble Savages been deprived for four long years when a remedy for their ills was but a two or three day journey away? What other marvels and amenities had the Preeminent One and his ministers deemed heretical, to the detriment of the Noble Savages? And the most insidious and dangerous question of all, if the Infinitude had seen fit to give Home a boon from the civilized world, was that not an indication that the time had come for the Noble Savages to give the civilized world the gift of the Universal Infinitude?

Not that a new schism disrupted Home. Both sides played a devious game. The Civilizers quietly sought converts but in other wise kept their heads low, for experience taught that the majority of the Noble Savages could be swayed easily against them. The authorities, for their part, could ill afford the Civilizers free rein but in like wise dared not declare open warfare on them for fear of giving credence to their philosophy. The authorities' strategy, for they were not stupid men, was to foment rumors that turned the Civilizers' very existence to their detriment by naming them as the cause for any adversity and making them appear to be a dark and malignant force that contended with the Universal Infinitude.

David remained aloof from the discord that winter, but was drawn into the thick of things the next spring when the father of a girl who was to marry the son of a Civilizer sequestered her in his cabin during the Feast of Fecundity. Distraught, the young man sought David's advice. David appealed to the Preeminent One, only to be accused of meddling, stripped of his post with the Guards, and assigned to New Rousseau where he could be watched. Two weeks later, in contravention of tradition, the girl was given to the son of the Chief Guard and caused a scandal when she and her true love became Wanderers and were caught, caged, and subjected to the Smoke of Retribution. From that day, disgusted by the intransigence of the authorities, David gave his allegiance to the Civilizers and became one of the leading figures in their cause.

Unaware of the silent battle being fought for their minds and souls, the peasants were even more caught up in the throes of religious fervor. I have ever thought warfare a stupid enterprise, but now understand it may sate a blood thirst natural to man, for after a century devoid of strife the whole of the Noble Savages' lives revolved around the three festivals and especially the third, wherein they murdered the Scapeweed Goat and his Ewe. As for the mechanism that prompted any person to seek to become addicted to a nefarious drug that made him a murderer and thenceforth to suffer ridicule, shame, derision, and an utterly ignominious death, that is as far beyond me as the reasoning that brings the morning sun and holds the moon in its place. Such was the desire of many of the young Noble Savages tho, and it was looked on with perfervid approbation by the vast majority of the remainder of that civilization, if civilization it may be called.

David and his fellow Civilizers watched with horror and a

sense of helplessness. Their every instinct told them their world had gone awry but, like a man who has lost the reins of a runaway team, they dared not jump out and could only hang on for the ride come what may. Not even when the Preeminent One deemed that any man or woman proved to be a Civilizer would suffer the Smoke of Retribution did they dare jump, but only held on the tighter and feigned their loyalty the more fervently. None but David was equipped to escape, given the increased vigilance of the Guards, and he held even more tenaciously tho with growing dismay to his dream of rescuing his son and restoring that unfortunately deluded youth to a semblance of sanity.

And then followed a blow that sent David reeling and pro-pelled him to desperation, for during the very spring of which I write, at about the same time K and I were striking out for the wilderness, David's son announced that the time was ripe for him to become an Aspirant. David heard the news at second hand and, tho he and his son had become somewhat estranged, sought him out in private.

The two men met in a secluded grove near the Field of Honor. David arrived early and sat upon the ground enrobed in his Mantle of Feathers and watched his son approach and sit down facing him. How much his son had grown had es-caped him, he said, and he was shocked. In his mind he saw a babe with a foot no longer than a man's little finger, a pudgy baby who smiled and cooed and played catch if you can with his toes. In his mind he saw a lad of five wrestling with a puppy, crying when he stubbed his toe on a rock, gleeful as he rode on his father's shoulders and caught at low hanging leaves. In his mind he saw a boy of nine at his side as they tramped thru the countryside from farm to farm, his gleaming body emerging from a pool after their morning toilet, his round face suffused with awe as he sat before a fire and listened to bedtime stories, his soft, sweet countenance innocent in sleep.

And in reality, he faced a lean man whose body was hard

and whose eyes glittered with purpose. A man who had left his father as every boy must, but one who had also become as unlike his father as a frog is a tadpole, and David's heart sank, for he enjoyed little hope of success in what he knew must be his last attempt to rescue his son, this boy turned man he loved in spite of all that separated them.

"You wished to see me, Father," said the son, paying cold deference.

The formal "you" that was used only for strangers or enemies tore thru David's heart like a knife, but he smiled. "Dost remember," he asked, "how we walked from farm to farm and sometimes made our camp by a stream, and how I told thee stories of thy mother and the olden days ere thou slept?"

"That was many years ago, Father. I am a man grown now and need no stories to help me sleep."

"Aye," agreed David. "A man grown. And a fine one too. Soon to be an Adept like thy forebears."

"Soon to be an Aspirant," his son corrected without a blink. "And a Scapeweed Goat if that be my privilege."

David sighed. "And so save the Noble Savages from what destiny fate hath decreed."

"And so fashion fate after our own will," said his son with a harshness that took David aback. "Do you doubt it?"

"Aye," said David. "I do."

"Father!" Numbed by David's announcement, his son looked around to see if any man might be in ear shot, and kissed his closed fist in the circle made by his thumb and forefinger. "Hast sunk so deep in apostasy?"

"Aye again," said David, his heart in his throat. "And would drag thee, my beloved son, to the depths with me that thy life mought be spared."

"A Civilizer!" exclaimed David's son, his face as slack in awe and fear as it had been when he listened to the tales of wild and dangerous spirits that roamed the wilderness. "My father is a Civilizer!"

"And would be a Wanderer too," said David with the determination of a man about to plunge into an icy stream. "With my son at my side, will he accompany me."

"Thou wilt be caged and breathe the Smoke of Retribution!"

"No, and neither will I allow thee to be, for I ken the ways of the Guards and am skilled in their arts." Daring hope, he held out his hand to touch his son. "Come with me. Wander with me to a new life where dost not have to murder or condone murder, to become a sacrifice to a God become so thirsty for blood that He is an abomination to any sensible man. I adjure thee! Come and wander with me while there is yet breath in thy body and thou canst see and taste and feel."

David's son stared at his father for a long moment, then shuddered with revulsion and shrank from his touch as one might from a ghost. "I will not," said he in a hollow voice, and then, strengthening, "I will not!"

"I have tried then," said David. "I have tried and thou hast listened. Very well then. Very well. Go thy way, then, my son, and I will go mine."

"No!" exclaimed his son. Rising, he spoke more as to a stranger than a father, and in a voice thick with righteous contempt. "I will be an Aspirant, and am determined to be the Scapeweed Goat as well. And as every good father who is an Adept, you will honor me by giving me with your own hand the Liquor of the Aspirants, and click your tongue five times in approbation when I drink of it."

"That I cannot do," said David, weighted down with a great sadness of spirit.

"That you will do!" retorted his son. "Or be caged like a common heretic and breathe the Smoke of Retribution, for unless you give me your word upon the instant that you have mended your ways, I swear upon my faith that I will inform upon you and click my tongue five times in approbation when you fall lifeless to the floor of your cage, for you will be my father no longer!"

March 3

𝕒𝕧 My missing hand did not lie. It rained yesterday and melted down a foot or more of snow before freezing again last night. This morning everything in sight is covered with a glaze of ice that shines with a brilliance beyond the eye's ability to endure for long. The ice will melt soon lest I miss my guess, for the sky already is clear and the sun warm on my skin when I go outside. Early winter, early spring, which bodes well since I am out of berries and very low on grain.

I am reminded when I look at my stump of a man who upon observing an old friend's new wife commented on her ugliness. "That is nothing," said the friend. "You should see her mother." And so it is with my stump. Red here and white there, lumpy on the edges and smooth over the protruding bone, it is a raving beauty when compared to its mother the hand, which I am well rid of.

"You will be my father no longer." No words had ever struck David harder. So great was the pain that he could have wished his breath might fail, for he loved his son with all his heart and soul.

A father who is no longer a father! No prospect can be more drear, as I well know. For a long moment David was stricken with a perturbation and heaviness of the mind that threatened to unman him, and it was not without a struggle that he recovered his senses and gazed up at his son and met his eye. "Very well," said he. "I will not be disowned by my son. Hast my word. I will administer the draught to thee and click my tongue five times in approbation."

His son murdered, and a murderer too if he had his way. The thought festered like an ugly wound. Behind him in the

Field of Honor lay the sad graves of those who had lost their lives in their desire to become the Scapeweed Goat, and David thought he heard their voices mewing like a chorus of lost kittens in their dismay at having been cut down so young. That he had championed that cause as a youth gave him no small amount of pain. That he had questioned it for twenty years consoled him but little, for he had nurtured his doubts in silence and so helped drown the mewing kittens whose voices would not be stilled.

He had had such dreams and now all were dashed, and tho the time had passed that he might save his son, he felt a growing determination to at least save him from the worst. To that end he rose at last and made his way to a small ravine he knew, where in the deep shadows he would find the roots from which were distilled the Potion of Expiation.

The Feast of Fecundity was to be held on a Thursday that year, and the first of the peasants began to gather in New Rousseau on the preceding Saturday, the day after David's conversation with his son. Each day more arrived. Men led bullocks and other stock to trade, women carried chickens and baskets of yams and potatoes and onions and carrots left over from the winter. Campsites sprang up everywhere, and fires blazed deep into the night as families and friends who saw little of each other during the year gathered to gossip, court, and disport themselves for the last time before the long months of spring and summer work. The smell of meat cooked over hot coals, of roasting yams, of baked onions and carrots in sweet milk, of fresh bread, and of nuts roasting in honey lay like an aromatic blanket over New Rousseau. Bright eyed children played, the girls giggling, the boys serious in mock combat and juvenile feats of speed and strength.

David lived two lives in the midst of this clamor, the first at night when he put aside his Mantle of Feathers and mingled in the guise of a peasant with his fellow Civilizers. Meeting secretly, they laid their plans in low whispers. Later, when the fires had died and the village slept, they skulked by ones and twos from shadow to shadow and hurriedly completed the tasks they had set for themselves, for time was of the essence.

By day David was the very model of propriety. He wore his mantle and walked with a stately air. He greeted old friends and smiled graciously and accepted the unending compliments and congratulations due the father of an Aspirant to Be. He saw his son twice, once on Sunday at the service held on Discovery Promontory, and the second time at the banquet held in the central meeting hall the night before the Blessing of the Aspirants and the Feast of Fecundity. On this august occasion, David sat across the table from his son and ate heartily and laughed and was witty until the benediction when he raised his eyes in prayer and saw a tuft of straw protruding thru a crack in the ceiling. And tho no one in attendance remarked on it, he later crept back in the early morning hours to remove the telltale sign before the mothers and sisters of the Aspirants to Be arrived at dawn to begin the ritualistic cleansing that transformed the central meeting hall into a holy temple.

The morning of the day of the Feast of Fecundity dawned bright and clear. David had slept no more than an handful of hours each night for the past week, but woke alert and infused with energy. New Rousseau was abuzz with the arrival of latecomers. The temple crawled with women scrubbing the floors and benches and long tables and setting out the myriad spring flowers brought to them from all corners of the valley.

No day of the year was happier for the Noble Savages. The Aspirants to Be, full of camaraderie for the last time, proceeded to the lake where they bathed in water blessed by the Preeminent One. The mothers and sisters of the Aspirants to Be were feted by the other women, who lay colorful robes on their sisters' shoulders and entwined garlands of spring flowers in their hair. The Adepts met in secret conclave to mix and bless the Liquor of the Aspirants that would be served that night in holy ceremony. The Guards brought in wooden kegs of the Drink of Pleasure, the mild infusion of 'scapeweed that the Noble Savages would later imbibe. Hourly the tension rose as the evening neared.

The Blessing of the Aspirants was a simple but moving ceremony. Each Aspirant to Be, wearing only a breech clout and a garland of holly in his hair and with his body freshly maimed and painted in gay colors, set out from his house or lodging as the sun sank below the hills. With his father or sponsor and his brothers at his side and trailed by his mother and sisters, he carried to the temple a torch symbolizing the light cast by the Universal Infinitude, and there set it in a sconce on the wall behind him. When all were arrived, the assembled Noble Savages waiting outside parted their throng to allow the Preeminent One and the procession of Adepts to pass thru it and enter.

David was frightened for the first time. The vials he had secreted in his robes, which were identical to those he and his fellow Adepts had filled that morning, dragged him down with their weight tho each was no heavier than a lark's egg. His breath was short, his mouth dry. Each step required an effort almost beyond his strength. Nowhere he cast his eyes could he find a single one of his co-conspirators.

The temple was ablaze with light, the air heavy with the cloying scent of flowers and perfumes mixed with the paints decorating the skin of the Aspirants to Be. A low murmur from the spectators sounded like a roar in David's ears. Nearly swooning, he listened to the Preeminent One invoke the Spirit of the Universal Infinitude. And then, as if a door had closed to shut out the world, a calm descended on him and his fears abated, and he gazed tenderly upon the young man whom he loved more than life itself, and listened to his son declare his intentions.

"My son was beautiful," said David in a voice lowered to a whisper by the effects of the poison in his system. "He was tall and comely. His body glowed as if infused with an inner light that escaped thru his eyes. I saw in him the babe and the child, the lad who walked and ate and slept with me and loved me with the simple, deep love a son may have for his father. Never had I loved him less, and never had I loved him more. He was my son, my soul, and my life."

David stopped for a moment, and when he continued, his voice was choked with sorrow. "My son was an Aspirant, too, a macabre and bloodied stranger. He was covered in gaudy paints in all the hues of the rainbow, and deep cuts beginning at the corners of his mouth raked upward across his cheeks like the whiskers of a mountain cat, and bled freely. And tho my heart cracked, my hand was steady as I substituted for the one handed me my secret vial filled with the Potion of Expiation, the vial that I had blessed with my own words even as the Preeminent One had blessed that other, and opened it and poured it into my son's bowl, and bade him raise it high and drain it to the dregs, and clicked my tongue five times in approbation."

March 4

The sun shone all yesterday afternoon, which melted the layer of ice covering the snow, as I predicted. Not a cloud in the sky today, and the sun has been warm. I kept a watch thru my glass on the upper reaches of the path that leads out of this prison valley, and believe I saw a patch of bare ground before the sun went down. Give me another four or five days like yesterday and I will eat my peaches and make my escape tho I must be cautious of floods from the rapid melt, but in any case prefer them to scurvy and slow starvation.

Would I have killed my son under those circumstances? I have talked with men who have told me I was a fool not to jump off the train careening down the mountain's side, for to ride was more dangerous than to leap. They were not there tho, and I was not with David, so I cannot judge if it was better for him to murder his son than to allow his son to be a murderer. He did in any case, and thought he was right at the time.

His son's raising and draining his bowl had been the signal for the other conspirators to act, and when nothing happened during the next few seconds, David worried that they had been discovered and their plot foiled. At last, it could not have been as long as a minute, he saw from the corner of his eye a small fire blossom in a nearby tree and one, two, and three arrows fly toward the temple, where he could only hope that one entered the hole cut in the roof and set afire the straw hidden in the ceiling.

He was not the only one to spot the arrows. Some in the gathered throng saw them and their companions from another tree on the opposite side of the temple, and raised the cry of fire.

And then one event followed so nearly on the heels of another that it was difficult to recount them in sequence. Confederates mingling in the throng outside set up the cry that the Guards were to blame, tho they were innocent. Three arrows flew through a window. Two struck the Chief Guard in his chest and throat when he leaped in front of the Preeminent One and killed him instantly, and the third killed an elderly Adept . Like cattle in a slaughterhouse when the smell of blood washes over them, the crowd outside bellowed in fear and ran into and trampled one another. Inside, the dazed celebrants ran from one side to the other in a panic that swelled when

David's son clutched his throat with one hand and pointed at David with his other. "My father hath slain me! He is a Civilizer! Slay him!" he cried out, and pitched forward onto his face.

Havoc supplanted the orderly procession of ritual. The Civilizers' ploy having worked, the milling cattle outside turned into a mob intent on annihilating the Guards, who put their backs together in small knots and drove off their assailants. The Aspirants to Be, who had been so intent on dying bare moments earlier but had not considered fire as their executioner, rushed to escape. Alone among the celebrants, David remained calm as the fire in the dry straw ate thru the ceiling and pieces of burning wood dropped like red and orange blossoms. He had just removed the second vial from his robe and was about to drink it down when his arm was struck from behind, which was the last he remembered of that night.

The sun was in his eyes and his head hurt when he awoke the next morning. He could not move his right arm, which was numbed. He had lost his Mantle of Feathers and wore only a breech clout that was soaked and fouled with his own urine and excrement. He was lying in one of the cages used to administer the Smoke of Retribution, which was made like those David had helped me build to hold feral pigs, viz. of stout sticks tied together with tough vines that had been soaked so they could not be unknotted but must needs be cut. One Guard, a sullen youth with a bruised and swollen face and more nearly asleep than awake, sat nearby to watch over him. And not an hundred feet away lay a mound of steaming ashes and blackened timbers that were the remains of the central meeting hall and holy temple.

Home slept. No people moved about, nor even a dog. The birds and cocks that should have been singing and crowing were silent. David's mouth was dry, and he had to swallow before he could speak to ask for water. For answer the Guard drank from a jug lying at his side, recorked it, and set it behind him.

There was no escape from the sun. David stood to stretch himself, but quickly growing faint huddled in a corner away from his excrement. And still Home slept, and the Guard sat motionless, and David sank into a torpor engendered by pain and thirst and heat and the utter hopelessness of his situation.

"They woke me with water," he went on, sipping some himself. "When I cleared my eyes and came to my senses, I looked up to see the Conclave of Adepts standing in front of my cage."

I have seen clergy aroused to righteous indignation, and they may rightfully be feared when in that state. Having been one of them tho, and desiring his own death in any case, David listened without consternation as the Preeminent One informed him that he and various other of his confederates, as soon as they were captured, would be executed en masse by the Smoke of Retribution. In the meantime he was to be permitted food and water, for they wanted him in good health so that he might fully enjoy his death.

No day, David said, ever dragged on longer or passed more quickly. Crowds of Noble Savages gathered to taunt and curse him, and cheer as new cages and prisoners arrived. By day's end six cages sat in a circle, and in each of the other five was a friend who had sought freedom in Civilization but would find it instead in death.

Bonfires lit the sky that night and the mood of the Noble Savages was ugly as they prepared for the next day's mass execution, which was scheduled for the moment the sun rose over Discovery Promontory. The Civilizers huddled in their cages. David's fellows took what comfort they could in each other but were loath to speak to him, for they had not been privy to his singular plan and were appalled by his murder of his own son.

"Even they, who should have understood my anguish, forsook me," David related. "All I had done, first in defense of Home and then to make it a better place thru purging and change, had been for naught. And within me grew a great and raging hatred by which I would have destroyed the whole fabric of our society if I could have. I knew nothing of Civilization, only that it must needs be better than the world we had constructed for ourselves, and that the Noble Savages would be better off joined with it rather than left to their own devisings."

Even then, before our great Civil War and the myriad other means by which I have observed that man may visit inhumanity on man, I knew enough of the foibles of Civilization to tell David how wrong he was. But since he was dying, I saw little point in bespoiling his dream, and let him continue his tale.

It was perhaps an hour before the cock should crow when an arrow from the darkness killed the Guard on duty. Within seconds a dozen Civilizers ran into the clearing and began hacking at the vines securing the doors of the cages that held their friends. No one ever having said, however, that the Guards were stupid, the Civilizers' vision of success was short lived. For even as David's door swung open, a host of Guards appeared out of nowhere and surrounded the clearing.

Why David ran or how he made his escape was unclear to him. He ran, he said, because the others ran and he was caught up in the general pandemonium. He made his escape by a fluke of luck, slipping between two Guards whose attention was distracted simultaneously. Incredibly, it was some time before the general alarm sounded to wake the population, and by then he had supplied himself with a peasant's vest. Part of him was pulled back to the center of New Rousseau to pay for the death of his son. Another part of him, the more sensible part, made his way farther and farther toward the edge of town by the simple expedient of avoiding people as they came out of doors to see what was the matter, and ducking unobtrusively from shadow to shadow until he was alone and running across the fields to the east.

Dawn found him climbing the path to Discovery Promontory. He was rested from his enforced stay in the cage. He had found food in the empty houses of peasants who had gone to New Rousseau for the Feast of Fecundity. "And dost thou know what I did?" he asked with a weak laugh. "Ran. After six years of teaching myself how to flee wisely, I fell into a panic and ran thru the woods like a stag being chased by hounds, stopping neither for food nor drink, sliding down cliffs, crashing thru brush."

He stopped and took my hand in his. "Never forget, friend J, that thy practical thoughts are but poor weak relatives to emotions, and especially to fear. Be ever on thy guard against this weakness that I had succumbed to, until I tripped and fell full length on my face in an icy stream, and came up sputtering and coughing but awake at last to my folly."

From the wish to die to the wish to live is but a step. David did not well understand his conversion, but knew that he had taken that step and wanted more than anything to find the Civilization he and his confederates had dreamed of, and bring it to Home that the Noble Savages might be turned from the aberrant path they had taken, and that his son's death might have some little value. How close behind him the Guards might be he knew not, only that he had left a trail they could follow with ease.

As I turned the snow that was my downfall to my advantage, so David turned his flight to his. The Guards were accustomed to panic stricken flight and would regard his capture as a simple task, which would relax their vigilance. His one hope then was to double back on his tracks, and the farther the better before they passed him. With any luck he would have some hours to reenter Home, and as much as a day to escape from the other side with more diligence.

His flight that time was calculated. As clumsily as an army

on a march, he left a clear trail down the stream until it met
another and then, becoming an Indian, carefully backtracked
past the point where he had originally entered the water, dried
himself off, and paralleled his original line of flight, only in the
opposite direction. Sure enough, before he had covered a mile
he heard the Guards who, never expecting him to be moving
toward them, were talking and joking in their confidence. It
was he, tho, who laughed silently as they passed beneath him
some five paces to his right and never guessed his presence.
An hundred breaths after their voices disappeared, he descended from his tree and continued, satisfied that the Guards
would lose his trail near the fall of night, at about the same
time he arrived at Discovery Promontory. From then on the
advantage was totally his, for he could steal unseen across
Home, sleep a few hours, and escape to the west. When the
Guards resumed their search for his spoor at dawn, he would
be well on his way and could hope, after a few days of easy
travel, to find Civilization.

"And yet," said I, "you came to us in a sore state, and near
death."

"Aye," David admitted with what I thought was another
chuckle. "But not, at least, from stupidity. From an accident,
rather, when I fell down a cliff and gave myself the wound that
was on my head. And from which thou and thy beautiful K
saved me, to thy own grave detriment." Again his hand
squeezed mine and held on tight. "Their deaths hang heavy on
my soul, J. Truly, I am culpable. Mine is deserved."

Tho secretly agreeing with him, I could not say as much to
a dying man. "You did not seek to do us harm, David," said I
instead. "I will avenge your death as well as hers and the
babe's."

"No need. Vengeance will not bring back K, nor the babe.
As for me, it is enough that thou recallest thy oath. So go
home, friend J. Go home. If Civilization is as kind and generous as thou and thy beautiful K . . . "

His voice faltered, and I could feel him struggle for breath as a spasm shook his poor frame. "David?" said I in the unearthly silence that followed. "David?"

"Thy hand in mine, Matthew," he whispered, addressing his son, I supposed, but gripping my fingers the more tightly. "Thy hand in mine, and we shall wander together forever-more."

So saying, he exhaled once, and his hand fell from mine to the floor, and he expired.

March 5 (Noon)

Has there ever been a more beautiful morning? The sun is shining brightly, the sky is the deep blue of a mountain lake. I am shirtless, the color of mare's milk, and Andrew and I are sitting on the porch to take the sun, especially on my stump. I had hoped to eat my peaches tonight and try to leave tomorrow, but that was wishful thinking. Three or four more days of this weather is all I ask, that I might effect my escape and bring my ordeal to an end.

My child dead before he could see the world into which he was born, my wife dead after only seventeen summers of her own particular beauty. David, too, dead before he should see the Civilization about which he was so misinformed. I will say this, tho. However mistaken he was about the beauty, bounty, or beneficence of Civilization, it beats starving or freezing to death alone in the mountains.

Nothing could have been further from my mind on that long ago night. How much of the night had passed I had no idea for the action and excitement that had been packed in it, nor how much remained as I could not see the stars. My only recourse was to sit and wait until my doorway should lighten. That and take care not to sleep. So I filled the dragging hours with thoughts of how I would kill the remaining Guard and, after I had buried my wife and David, strike out for Home, which I was determined to find, and there wreak a terrible vengeance.

My first problem was to get outside without being killed on the spot, for the Guard could wait for me anywhere, even just outside the door. I had, then, to find some advantage by which the odds might be evened.

I was confident he would not play the fool and enter my cabin after the certain death of his fellows there. Consequently reasoning that I had time, I climbed quietly into the loft and extracted some more chinking from underneath the eaves so, with the help of my mirror, I could see along the west side of the cabin. Likewise on the east I had but to enlarge the holes thru which passed the ropes that had earlier held the log suspended there.

Dawn came more quickly than I expected. One minute all was dark, the next my door stood out clearly. Soon I could plainly see the willow brake at the south end of our valley, and then the leaves turning golden as the rising sun struck them. That same sun was my informant, for I could see thru the chink under my eaves the long pole of the shadow of a man extending past the west side of my cabin. Since I could see no similar shadow on the porch, I knew the Guard waited for me outside my door to the right.

My first impulse was either to sneak out thru the hole David had used the night before or to dive across the porch and shoot him before he should have a chance to recover from his surprise, but David's admonitions about the Guards' wariness disabused me of those notions. Instead, I took my time to devise a safer plan, and after I had worked it out to my satisfaction, played upon his nerves some by honing my knives so he would know I was inside. At last, there being no sense in waiting any longer, I removed my boots and slung them around my neck on their strings, stuffed my pistol in my belt and, as quiet as Andrew is when he watches me write, removed the pot from the hook in the fireplace and climbed up the inside of the chimney.

I could see my shadow on the ground as I emerged from the top. Quickly, and praying the Guard was not looking that way, I squeezed out the hole and climbed down the outside. It was but a matter of a moment to slip on my boots, for I did not wish to stupidly lose the day by stepping on some stray Wasp of Death. And then, recalling David's description of the Weaving Dance, I kept the cabin between my adversary and myself until I reached our well, where lay one of the Guards David had slain. From there I carefully and silently circled toward the front of my cabin, and the confrontation that would end in either the Guard's death or my own.

The Guards, as I think on them, must have taken their lessons from the carnivores, which often lie in wait for hours for their prey. This one, I shortly saw, stood as motionless as a statue at the corner of the cabin, with his back to me and facing the doorway. Careful not to look at him directly, for a man knows as well as an animal when he is being watched, I continued until I reached the spot I wanted, which was in deep grass some fifty paces behind him. And then it was my turn to play the carnivore and to rattle his nerves in order to shake his confidence when the moment of truth arrived.

Hatred can be a heady emotion and may even be exhilarating when fear is mixed in with it. I had seen first hand how ferocious and fearless the Guards might be, and had heeded well the stories David told me. I had buried my son, ministered to my wife, and watched her die. I had killed another handful of men and waited to kill my first while looking him in the eye for I was determined he should see whence came his death, and understand the malice and hatred I felt for him.

I saw when he felt the weight of my stare on his back, for his right shoulder and his head, theretofore motionless, jerked slightly, whereupon I dropped to my belly quickly and lay unmoving in the grass where I could see him but he could not see me. Directly, a quizzical expression on his face, he dared a quick look, then a long, searching stare from side to side. There being nothing to see, he returned to his vigil, but I could sense a tension in his shoulders that I had not seen before. I gave him an hundred breaths, and then rose and again subjected him to my stare, and only barely dropped into the grass when he whirled as if he had heard a sound.

He knew someone was there, and knew as well that I was trapped in the cabin, for he had heard me honing my blades earlier. He knew he was in danger, and yet could not tell from what. At last, tentatively, as if trying to discern how he should watch his front and rear at the same time, he turned back toward the door. And it was then that I rose and, pulling my pistol, said, "When nine men cannot kill two, they must indeed be fools who have no more brains nor sense than slow and stupid oxen."

I will give him credit. How I had gotten out he did not know. That he had been tricked was no doubt an embarrassment, but he wasted no time on self recriminations, instead he immediately turned and strode toward me. I let him close the gap between us by half before I extended my arm and, exactly as David had told me not to, aimed at him and squeezed off one shot to see what he would do. True to David's word, the Guard seemed to flow to the left, then stopped, and displayed such an evil smile as I have never before or since seen on the face of man.

"Who calls another man a fool does so at his own grave peril," said he in a gravelly voice. "You should have been content to die quickly and have only your head carried back. Now I will drive you before me like a beast and you will die eleven deaths, one for each of my fellows you have killed, and each more terrible than the one preceding." With that, he opened a small bag hung at his waist and dropped into it what I took to be a handful of the Wasps of Death, pulled a short club from a band tied around his thigh, and came at me.

The Weaving Dance was an apt name. In all my years I have seen its like employed only in San Francisco by some natives of Corea who had brought their methods from the Far East to that city. Now here and now there, the Guard looked like a ghost of himself in three places at once. My arm still outstretched, I fired once more with no more effect than shooting at the moon. Finally, remembering in the nick of time, I lowered my arm in order to aim from my waist, threw up my left arm to distract his attention, and thereupon shot him three times in the belly.

I do not care how strong a man is. Three balls from a .40 caliber pistol at five paces will knock him down. And so it was that the Guard stopped in his tracks and sat down with his legs splayed in front of him, and stared in disbelief at the blood gushing from his belly.

"Twelve," said I, placing my revolver on cock, for I had one round left. "And an hundred more before I am finished, for every one of you who ever walked is not worth a tenth the value of my wife and son."

And so saying, I put him out of his misery with a final shot to the head.

March 5 (Night)

Hope springs eternal in the human breast, it is said. It has sprung a veritable torrent in mine today, for the weather holds. Andrew and I took a stroll down the trail from my cabin to the floor of the valley this afternoon. That path is clear enough, but the first two or three hundred feet of the trail out of here are totally impassable. We had gotten halfway home when I heard a loud crack like the report of a buffalo gun. A second later, before my eyes, a slab of rock the size of my cabin broke off the mountain and, falling like a great cleaver, chipped a thick chunk of ice off the middle fifty feet of the clogged part of the trail, and landed where we had been standing only minutes before.

I confess, now that my luck has changed and my salvation lies but two or three days ahead, that I was less than honest when I said I did not fear death. But does any man not fear death? I have read that Indians face death with equanimity, but experience has taught me otherwise. Else why should they contend so fiercely against that grim reaper? As for me, tho my time will surely come as it must for any man under the sun, I am glad to say it will not be soon or in this valley. The spirit was right. It is not my time yet.

I will also say this. When I was a young man, and even until ten years ago, I should have laughed in death's face. Not now. I have learned that death is no clown and that challenging it is not a game to be played in order to alleviate boredom.

A good day's work awaited me before I should begin my journey of vengeance. First I ate since, I was surprised to discover, I was famished. My wife, who was laid out, I wrapped in our best quilt, a double wedding ring pattern of many colors, and spoke to her of my sorrow and our love as I dug her final resting place in the same spot where our son lay. Then laying his poor form in her arms, I enfolded them together in the earth that will one day enfold us each and every one, and said my prayers over them and commended them to God, in whom I still believed. That finished, I dug another hole nearby and, tho I could not explain myself and felt silly doing so, held a cup of water to David's lifeless lips and kissed my closed fist at the circle made by my thumb and forefinger, as he had over K, before covering him too. As for the Guards, I let them lie where they had fallen for the vultures and wolves and feral pigs to feed on.

A fool's errand is not always embarked upon in a foolish manner. Indeed, I was the very model of a rational man, and set about my preparations with more single minded purpose than is required for my escape from this valley. The Guards in their efficiency had slaughtered my horses, cow, and pigs. The chickens still lived tho, so I killed them and also cut some of the good haunch meat from my cow. Then I cooked my meat and added to the coals some new potatoes I dug. When all had cooled, I made a pack of the meat and potatoes and two loaves of bread so I should have food without a fire for the next week.

No soldier or Indian scout was ever better prepared. I wore buckskins so I should blend into the forest, moccasins so I should walk quietly, an old slouch hat to shed the rain and disguise the shape of my head. On and about myself I carried my revolver and my spare loaded cylinders in a bag, my broad and narrow knives sheathed, a well balanced tomahawk an Indian friend had given me and that I always carried whilst in the wilderness, and my rifle, powder horn, and shot bag. Added to these warlike accoutrements were a blanket and an oiled cloth and my sack of food tied in a roll that I slipped over my shoulders and could loose in a second. When I was finished, which was near sundown, I walked away from our valley without looking back, found a safe spot in the woods, and lay down to sleep.

Of my journey I can think of nothing of note save that when the trail bent to the north and east, whence we had come, I struck off cross country directly east, where I supposed I should find Home. As for my thoughts, they were no more original or exciting than the plodding repetitive motion of my feet. Images of my dead son, images of my dead wife and our short history together, and images of David and dead and dying Guards. To what end I do not know, for even in those days I knew that vengeance does not revitalize the dead, and serves no purpose. All it has ever brought me is a heavier emptiness than I felt before I exacted recompense for whatever wrong I suffered. And yet the desire for vengeance may overpower reason with a logic of its own, which is what happened when I set the trap for the gluttons and paid for it with my hand.

A man who knew his destination and needed not fear the Guards could have made the journey in three days. I would have taken seven were it not for a stroke of luck, by which on the morning of the sixth day I chanced to hear a voice ahead of me and, hurrying quietly forward and climbing a tree, witnessed a trio of Guards heading north and then turning back to the east.

David had told me that the Guards left no trail, and indeed I had seen nor hide nor hair of one tho I supposed them to have frequented those parts, but finding some in the flesh was a different matter entirely. Consequently, for they evidently supposed themselves safe in their own back yard and did not keep watch to the rear, I was able to follow them. Less than an hour later they hit a well used trail and two hours after that met up with some of their fellows when the trail they were on crossed another.

I have ever walked stealthily in the wild, so I moved as close as I needed to hear them.

"Hast seen or heard anything?" asked one, whom from an armband he wore and the authority in his voice I took to be a commander.

"Nay. Nor sight nor sound."

The commander pursed his lips and looked directly past the tree that hid me. "Four days past their time. I like it not, lads. And three more days ere Harold and his fellows can return, unless he meet them on the way. I like it not."

The three scouts I had followed agreed.

"Very well then, lads." He nodded to an underling who handed the commander a leather bag. "Here's meat for ye. Return to the broken tree, take thy rest, and resume thy posts. Until tomorrow, then."

Andrew points out that I was very stupid not to have thought of their sending out scouts to discover what had happened to the overdue Guards, and I agree now as readily as I realized it then. Still, there was nothing to do but press on. I had, after all, at least three days of freedom before they began to look for me. So thinking, I waited until the six at hand were out of sight, then crossed the commander's tracks, left the path, and found a temporary haven in a windfall halfway down some hills that I immediately saw defined the western edge of Home.

The valley appeared much as David had described it. I could not see the southern end because a rain was falling there, but the lake was clearly visible and, on the far side, smoke came from buildings that I took to be New Rousseau. And less than a quarter mile below me and to my left lay a farm. So after I had rested and eaten, and being filled with curiosity, I set out for a closer look.

I have seen poor farms and poor people the wide country over, and they are identical for all their differences. The house was built of a beam frame filled with stone and mortar, and covered with a sod roof grown over with grass. The one window I could see on the south side was shuttered. A chimney identical to the one David had made for my wife and me rose

over the roof. The barn was like the long houses I have seen
that many Indian tribes build. Twenty paces long and eight
wide, it was constructed as I later learned of poles bent and
lashed at the top, and the whole covered with reed thatching,
which is not the best material for keeping out rats. Round
about the barn were a series of sties and corrals for livestock
and a long crib filled with corn. Chickens scratched in the dirt,
and a half dozen ducks lazed about on a small pond that was
covered with scum.

The family had no dog, else I might have been discovered.
I almost was in any case for, relieved by my safe arrival in
Home, I fell asleep. Near sundown I was awakened by voices
and, not daring move so much as a muscle, lay barely concealed as the farmer, his wife, and three children passed within
a dozen paces of me.

I could tell little of them on that first look, for each was
laden with a towering pile of hay which they carried into the
barn. Shortly the farmer emerged with a wooden wheel that he
and his son rolled past me as they retraced their steps to the
field whence they had come, and the woman and her two
daughters emerged from the other end of the barn and disappeared around the front of the house. A moment later the
shuttered window flew open. And then began my short lesson
in the daily life of the Noble Savages as observed from several
vantage points during the remaining hours of the day, which
no other living man that I know of has described.

Somewhere between Indian and white, the Noble Savages
appeared an industrious, clean, and happy race. The woman
and girls sang, laughed, and chattered as they went about their
chores. Their bodies were lithe and comely, not only all the
children's but the mother's and father's also, for theirs was not
an idle life. The woman's first task was to lay a fire in a stone
fireplace built under an open shed to the side of the house.
That done, she and the daughters stripped off their short skirts
and doeskin vests, which were the sum of the clothes they wore

and, laughing and cavorting about like playful lambs, bathed on a platform built near the well. When they had finished they dressed in nothing more than loincloths that concealed their genitals, which made the mother even more desirable than she had been completely naked. So much so that, in spite of the recent passing of my wife, my lust, to my shame, became immediately evident, had anyone been there to see.

Whatever carnal thoughts my inflamed brain harbored, they were stilled by the creak of wagon wheels and the softly spoken commands of the father. No sooner had I hid myself than a yoke of oxen pulling a quaint two wheeled wooden wagon hove into sight around the tree line. Since there was nowhere to sit, father and son stood side by side, and behind them lay the broken wheel they had replaced.

The males, like the females, wasted no time in getting down to work. The boy knew his jobs and set to cheerfully without a word from his father. The oxen were rubbed down with hands full of straw, put into their corral, and fed some grain to supplement the day's forage. The stock was watered and fed, and each one's body checked over carefully. The cart was cleaned and put inside the barn. Soon enough their chores were finished, and father and son took their turns on the bathing platform.

Whatever their race, the Noble Savages' children were raised more in the manner of Indians than whites, which is to say with a remarkable degree of freedom and love. For as they no doubt had worked hard all day, so too were they turned loose to play when the work was done. The mother cooking and the father taking his ease near her and occasionally lending a hand, the children ran about like spirited colts at tag and then, for the youngest girl, at a game of hide and go seek, which to her delight she was allowed to win.

I could not believe there was a mean bone in any of their bodies. I confess therefore that I found myself wondering if David had exaggerated his stories of the blood thirstiness of the Noble Savages. Not yet acquainted with some of the Plains Indians I later met, who were pure savages, I could not believe that children who worked willingly and played so unrestrainedly could participate in the bloody rites David had described, nor that men and women who were so demonstrably gentle and unabashedly devoted to each other and their children could murder their own kind in an orgy of passion. The simple family I watched was an island of tranquillity and beauty. Indeed, they lived as I had dreamed that my wife and I should live, a simple bucolic life in which we should have raised and nurtured our children and let them loose in the world so we could enjoy our sunset years in the peace of God.

It was then that bitterness flooded my soul and hardened my angry heart to stone. What right did those people have to such bliss? I asked myself. I should have been content with those oxen, those pigs and sheep and chickens. I should have labored long and hard for such a barn. I should have delighted in such a bathing platform, and my organ should have risen for no woman other than my wife, who was beautiful beyond compare in my sight, and utterly dear to me. And how I should have reveled in three little lambs of my own! It was if the man had stolen my wife, and together they had stolen my children and deprived me of my very life! They deserved death, and I more than any other man on earth deserved the satisfaction of bringing it to them.

Hatred is a ravenous beast, a mole or shrew that consumes thrice its weight in a day. How my hatred grew and bloated me! Every tender motion I interpreted as foul. Did the husband touch his wife on the breast and smile at her, I found it lewd and lascivious. Did a child run to her mother with a bruise, and the mother hold and caress her babe and gently kiss the spot and send her on her way, I found her concern loathsome. Did the boy run to his father to show him some little thing fashioned of twigs, and the father praise him and ruffle his hair, I found them fatuous and vile.

I would have killed them had I been given another hour. I laid my plans, knew how I would walk slowly toward them, how I would slay first the children and then the wife and last the father, steeped in horror and fear. I would have, had not suddenly the hairs on the back of my neck prickled and stood up straight. Scant seconds after I dropped silently to the ground and composed myself so they should not sense my presence from my emotions, three Guards and an Adept appeared on the same path the farmer had taken. They ran silently, not as if they were chasing some person or thing, but as a mode of travel, the same easy, loping run that Indians employ and that eats miles, with two of the Guards abreast preceding the Adept, and the third bringing up the rear.

The peasant family was taken as much by surprise as I, and their happiness and laughter dissolved on the instant. Immediately the girls hid behind their mother, who quickly donned a vest in order to conceal her breasts. The boy froze on the spot and, fear and pride warring in his tiny chest, valiantly stood his ground. The father, who had appeared arrogant to me, was transformed. Rising from his chair, he stepped out from under their dining shed and stood with his head bowed submissively like an abject ox about to receive a yoke.

I was close enough to hear and, being used to their language from having known David, could pick out at least the gist of their conversation. The Guards' immediate demand was for food. Hurriedly the mother and girls ran into the house and the boy caught up a chicken, which he slaughtered on the instant by snapping off its head. Within minutes it was cleaned and dressed and put on the fire, along with other edibles brought by the woman.

Tho I had thought the farmer arrogant, his arrogance was of my perception, as compared to that of the Guards and the Adept, which was real. They did not at first deign to so much as look at their hosts, and when they did talk to them, issued abrupt commands. Thus the father and son carried buckets of water to the bathing platform for them and, after the travelers had finished their evening toilet, the daughters brought them leaves from an herb which they rubbed themselves with. The mother served them clay cups which they sipped at while they relaxed on a long bench and waited for their suppers to cook.

No king, I think, was ever served more grandly than those four. A peremptory nod brought a pitcher to refill their cups. A brusk command, and the two little girls ran off to pull hands full of mint and used them to keep the flies off their guests and to sweeten the air, which I could tell because I had taken care to move upwind of them. All the while, the father stood ready to jump at their slightest gesture, by which I learned they could not be of any Indian race I knew, for no brave I had ever seen would so humble himself before even the greatest chief.

The sun had just set as the travelers finished their meal. Then it was I learned the reason for the peasants' discomfiture, for the Guards began a nasty interrogation of them while the Adept watched with what I could only call amusement.

A Civilizer, one who did not deserve to be called a Noble Savage, had disappeared from New Rousseau the night before and was presumed to have become a Wanderer. Indications were that the fugitive had taken a direction that led past the peasants' farm, and the Guards wanted to know if any of the five had seen a stranger that day. Obviously nervous, the husband explained that they had been employed the day long making hay, as the Guards had undoubtedly noticed when they passed thru the field to the south on their way to the farm. Any Wanderer would have seen them at work and, knowing that those who lived on the periphery of Home were bound to report the passage of strangers, circled around them. If such was the case, yes, a Wanderer could have crossed their land, but they had not seen him or her, whichever the case might be.

The answer sounded reasonable to me but did not satisfy

the Guards, who proceeded to question everyone individually. No one escaped. They bullied the children, left the little girls in tears when they roared terrible threats at them, and the boy cowed and shaken when they first tried to bribe him with the promise of a fine dog and then slapped his face until he fell down when he could not tell them what they wanted to know. The wife they browbeat and called vile names, told her she lied and that her children had told them she had fed the Wanderer, and gave up only when she haughtily told them that she was a free woman, the niece of an Adept, that she valued her honesty as she valued her life, and that they could do what they would for her children had said no such thing because they were not liars, and neither would she be to cover up the Guards' inability to do their job and catch a Wanderer.

The husband came in for the worst part, for while they evidently feared beating a woman, they were pleased to oblige a man. What impressed me most was not so much that they beat him, but that they did it skillfully, an evidence to me that they had had a great deal of practice. And it was then that my sympathies changed and my hatred for the farmer and his family dissolved and was turned against the Guards and the Adept.

Those simple people had told the truth. No child I have ever seen could have maintained such a complex web of lies as the Guards charged them with. The farmer and his wife cared not one whit for Wanderers or whatever else the Guards and Adept worried themselves with. They cared about and wanted only what simple people the world over have cared about and wanted since the beginning of time, which was their land and their livelihood and their children, their happiness and their love and their freedom. I had no argument with the farmer and his wife, nor had I reason to envy them. They were no threat to me and never had been.

The Guards and Adept were, tho, as have been the Guards and Adepts by whatever name they are known in any society I have ever seen. We call them clerics, police, generals, and politicians, and they are the greatest liars and connivers and instigators of hatred and evil in this world.

I can understand why men treat those of different races badly, because differences breed distrust and fear. But it escapes me entirely why they treat their own kind so badly, no better than animals, for you would think they would try to protect their own kind in an oft unfriendly world. And so it was that I realized the farmer was my brother and his wife my sister and his children my children. And that if death were to visit their farm that night, it would leave my brother and my sister and my children untouched. Their fear was as the blood of the lambs painted on the gateposts of the Israelites in ancient Egypt, and I, the avenging Lord, would pass over their house and slay their oppressors.

March 6 (Noon)

This would be a day for singing, had I a voice any better than a frog's. This world is, after all is said and done, a fine place to find oneself. I woke with a pleasant heavy stiffness in my member that I have not had for over a month, which is an omen I take to mean I am not destined to die until I have enjoyed at least one more woman in my lifetime. Since there are no women here, I am therefore meant to escape. In confirmation of this prediction, having fallen asleep last night to the sound of water dripping from my eaves, I woke to the same music magnified. In addition, there is not a single cloud in the sky, and the sun is already bathing the trail out of here. Andrew and I inspected the beginning of the trail again this morning. I would have returned, shouldered my pack, and left this morning were it not for the first hundred feet, which is still utterly impassable. I feel in my bones that it will be negotiable by tomorrow, but will wait until I see it again late this afternoon before I make my decision. Andrew is positive that tomorrow is too soon, but I flatter myself by thinking that is because he wants me to stay as long as possible, for he has decided to remain here rather than to venture into Civilization. When I tell him he would have made a good Noble Savage, he says that is not the reason. It is not that he fears Civilization but that he has no use for it, and would rather take his chances with hawks and owls and foxes and wolves than with people.

With only one or two more days to go, I am casting my last chips in the pot. The glutton came calling last night after I finished writing and I threw him a side of Duke's ribs. I do not know who was most surprised by this largess, the glutton, Andrew, or myself. Andrew chided me but quickly retired to his biscuit tin when I asked him if he had rather the glutton feast on Duke or on him. Luckily for him I am in good spirits, for I cannot stand sullenness, be it even in a mouse.

I am on my way out of here and can taste my freedom. A pot filled with the fattest part of Duke I could find and all but the last pound or two of my grain, which I will leave for Andrew, is bubbling away on my fire. I will eat well today in order to build up my strength in case I can leave in the morning. If not, there will be plenty left for tomorrow. The last I will take with me so I will have food on the trail. My pack is ready, and includes a small bag of gold nuggets to keep me until I can return for more. Glory hallelujah! Tonight, tomorrow at the latest, I will sit on my porch and savor my peaches.

And so I near the end of my tale, which I resume with four more Noble Savages taking their anonymous places on my list. They were easy prey, no doubt because almost an hundred years of security in the valley Home had lulled them against any danger there. Not wanting to shoot them and raise an alarm, I slit the Guards' throats as they lay side by side on a bed of hay just inside the barn door, and slipped my slim knife between the ribs of the Adept when he, alerted to the danger by the gurgling of the third Guard, woke and tried to flee. Keeping a short bow and a quiver of arrows from one of the Guards and the Adept's Mantle of Feathers to use as a disguise should I later need it, I let them bleed dry and buried them deep in the dried hay in the loft where the flies would not get to them and the dryness would keep them from smelling for a few days. The bloody straw they had slept on I scattered in the pig sties in the hope that it would be trampled by morning, and any traces of the murders destroyed so the farmer and his family would not be held culpable if questioned. My tasks accomplished, I retired to the windfall I had found earlier just as the sky began to lighten, wrapped myself in my blanket, and fell asleep.

Dull, leaden clouds hung low over the land when I woke that afternoon. Pleased with my exploits of the night before, I ventured out a little way to make sure I had left no spoor in the dark, then made myself comfortable and spent the rest of the day eating the last of my food and thinking about my wife and child. Near sundown the clouds broke, and the golden light slanting in from the west made the valley Home look like a veritable Eden. Knowing that it was a Hell instead, I filled my mind with dark thoughts and lay down to sleep until dark, when I should set out for New Rousseau.

I thought I should die on the spot when I woke some time later and discovered a blade at my throat. I was surrounded like the peddler David had told me about by six gray-painted Guards, with another dozen waiting in the wings in case I should escape the inner circle. I had at least, to judge from their number, earned their respect.

How they found me I could not imagine, for I had made no fire, had remained concealed, and could not, knowing where I had been, have tracked myself. Find me they did tho, and the bodies of the four I had killed, as I learned when they stripped me to the buff and, with separate ropes tied to each of my ankles, led me to the barn. There I was forced to remove the bodies from the hay and, receiving a lashing every time I misunderstood one of their commands, carry them to the washing platform and bathe them.

After washing the corpses and laying them out, I was forced to load them and my clothes and gear into the farmer's wagon, and then I was hitched like a mule or an ox to it and, lashed whenever I faltered or erred, driven up hill and down dale and around the lake to New Rousseau.

I survived that night because I was young and hale and blessed with a rugged constitution. They lashed and goaded me up the hills, laughed at and mocked me when the weight of the cart and its load pushed me down at a stumbling run. Fear gave way to hunger which in turn fell to thirst which dissolved in a fog of pain and fatigue. My feet were cut from rocks I could not see because of the darkness, and bled profusely. My sides and back were laid open by the lashings they had received, and stung the worse for the sweat that ran into each cut. So it was that, only hours earlier having anticipated with great good humor my surreptitious entry into New Rousseau, I was completely unaware of my public arrival there. Reduced to little more than a broken animal, I remember only being told to stop, looking up and seeing a blur of red and blue, and then the darkness of the earth rising to meet me.

David had been right about the Guards' tracking abilities, as I had learned to my chagrin, and right too about the Adepts' expertise with drugs. I vaguely recall being thrown into a cage and given some water and a thin gruel, which I suppose I drank down before fading into oblivion. When I woke it was morning, and I was so stiff and sore that I could scarce move and so hungry that my head swam. I drank down, therefore, the first cup they gave me, and ate without question when they slid a plate between the bars. The next I knew, the sun was going down and, to my amazement, the morning's stiffness was gone and my cuts were bandaged with leaves and poultices that made them half healed save for those on my feet, which were to take longer.

I was imprisoned in one of the execution cages that David had all too vividly described, which in turn was sequestered out of view of the general populace in a small courtyard made of woven mats. Three men, older Guards whom I took to be Traders from their ability to speak an English I could more easily understand, took turns around the clock watching over me. On the next two afternoons shortly before the evening meal, I was interrogated by a pair of Adepts who wanted to know who I was, whence I had come, and how much I knew about the Noble Savages. Not wishing to implicate any of David's family or friends, I made up a story about having discovered the valley by chance. The only questions I answered honestly were those about the farmer and his wife and children, and then I took care to exonerate them from any complicity with me.

I might as well have told the truth from the beginning, for they had deduced my identity on their own from the description of me given to them by the Guard who had returned to tell them where I lived. And so it was that on the third day after my capture I was handed the quilt in which I had wrapped my wife and babe, and told that I had arrived in Home only because I had taken a different route than had the Guards sent to discover why their nine colleagues had failed to reappear on time. This latter expedition had found my valley and the slain Guards, had dug up the graves of my wife and son and David, and had then followed my tracks back to Home, where they had arrived that morning. The game was up, and I was sentenced to death. Three nights hence, on the night of the harvest moon, I and a handful of Civilizers would breathe the Smoke of Retribution, not only to pay for our crimes, but also to whet the Noble Savages' appetites for the final act during the Feast of the Gesture of Propitiation, which was the Gesture of Propitiation itself, the death of the Scapeweed Goat and his Ewe.

Since I could see no way out of my predicament, I took pains, when confronted by him that same afternoon, to tell the Preeminent One what I thought of him and the Noble Savages' society, and that I was glad David had defeated them and saved his son from an ignominious death. I still see the Preeminent One in my dreams. A tall and probably once well built man, he was around sixty years of age and had gone to fat. He was, as David had told me, the fifth of his kind. A large goiter disfigured his neck and gave him the appearance of a monstrous toad with the unlikely but striking plumage of a red and blue bird that had got too old and fat to fly. Toad or bird, he had the eyes of a man and a shrewd one at that, and as he listened I could see in them consternation that I should know so much about the Noble Savages, then unwilling agreement with my declaration that the Noble Savages' way of life was doomed in any comparison with Civilization, and finally a maddening smugness in his conviction that his subjects should remain untainted, because he was bound of necessity to believe that his power could not be diminished nor his realm vanquished. As to whether or not he truly believed the Noble Savages' fabrications concerning the Universal Infinitude I could not tell, nor do I know to this day. I suppose that he did tho, even as our present politicians and clerics and generals believe the silliness they spout, else they could not convince so many others to support their policies, fill their purses, or fight their wars.

And now, my stew being cooked, Andrew and I will eat a bite, take a rest for an hour or two, and later walk down to the floor of the valley and look at the path leading out to see how the thaw is progressing.

March 6 (Night)

Better and better! Water is cascading down the side of the mountain and eating away at the ice that remains, and the temperature stands above freezing, tho it may drop later. No matter. The path should be passable late tomorrow. I would leave then if I had the slightest inkling of what the trail on the other side of the pass holds in store, but such a venture at night would be foolhardy with only one hand. Chomp at the bit as I may, it is none the less the better part of wisdom to wait until the next morning. All is in readiness for my departure, and I am a bundle of nerves with anticipation. It is a good thing that I have the end of this tale to fill the remaining hours, for it is difficult for a man with one hand to twiddle his thumbs, which is the only activity I should be left with.

Twiddling thumbs was, in fact, the sum of my activity in my prison cage those many years ago, for other than the interviews with the Adepts I was left alone to contemplate my fate. It is difficult for a man my present age to contemplate death, impossible for one only twenty. That is a strange thing I have never understood. Death was no more a stranger to me then than it is now. I had had two brothers and a sister who died. I had seen men die violently, for the frontier was no drawing room. My wife and child were dead, and David as well. I had killed no fewer than thirteen men myself. And yet, so well acquainted with death, I could not imagine my own.

I have faced death many times in the years since, and never with a second thought, for either it has rushed upon me unexpectedly and I have escaped its clutches by leaping aside or diving for cover the way a rabbit will when a hawk swoops on it, or I have evaded it by a mixture of stealth, cunning, strength, and bravado, whichever was necessary. That time tho, my first to feel the grim reaper's gown virtually wrapped around me, was an introduction to make later encounters pale in comparison, for I could neither leap nor dive, nor contrive by any means to escape my fate.

The night after my meeting with the Preeminent One was the hardest, for I had lost any hope of escape and was obsessed with the thought of a choking death in the Smoke of Retribution. Never have I felt so helpless. Outside the walls the air vibrated with excitement and anticipation as the Noble Savages gathered for the Feast of the Gesture of Propitiation. I could hear their laughter and their songs. I could hear drums beating and the plaintive piping of reed flutes. I could smell the smoke from their fires and the meat they cooked. And I could but stand and grip the bars of my cage, or lie diagonally across the floor, which was the only way I fit, and stare up at the small circle of brightness that was the moonlight shining thru the funnel. I tried to take comfort in the fact that they had paid dearly for my life, but their thirteen deaths to my one was meaningless. I sought solace in the hope that I would soon join my darling K and our child, but that hope failed me when compared with the certainty that I should cease to breathe or think or feel. It was with a heavy, heavy load on my soul that I at last fell into a troubled sleep.

"Man? Oh, wake up, man! Wake up!"

The soft calls roused me, and I waked to discover that my captors had removed the walls that surrounded me in order to place me on display. My cage sat nearby the ruins of the meeting hall David and his fellows had burned, which was being replaced by a new one that was finished save for a roof. The cries had come from seven unfortunate creatures imprisoned in cages like mine but some paces away from me.

"Who are you?" I asked, rubbing my eyes against the sunlight.

"They call us Civilizers, and doomed," said one man, whose bearing was regal even in capture.

"Then David did not exaggerate," said I. "They will kill every one of you they can catch."

David's name was a magic word, for no sooner had I said it than a hail of questions too thick to answer flew at me. "Didst know him?" "He is safe, then?" "He found a city? Thou art from a city?" "A civilized man! Do thy fellows follow thee? Will we be saved?"

"Wait. Wait!" cried I, trying to calm them. "David is dead at the hands of the Guards."

At that, one of the women wailed piteously and reached her hand across the open space to grasp that of a companion, who also wept.

Lame brained, I kicked myself for robbing them of the one hope they still had, that one of them had escaped, and was about to apologize when a dozen Guards ran around the corner of the building and began beating on the bars of the Civilizers' cages and ordering them to be still and not talk to me. And to ensure that we should have no further intercourse, they promptly wheeled my cage out of sight of theirs on the far side of the building, where I was placed on public display.

A king's ransom could not have bought them a finer object of curiosity and contempt. I was the personification of evil, the first representative of Civilization the general populace had seen. I had invaded their land and killed some of their number. Indeed, I looked like an exotic, newly discovered monster such as is found in our current bestiaries, for I was naked as a jay, bearded and hairier on my body than they, and filthy with mud and my own excretions. Only the addition of horns and a tail could have made me more alien and feared. And to my shame, I confirmed their expectations by acting like a pitted bear or caged ape, which made me the equal of a whole circus in one person.

Save for a band, which the Noble Savages lacked, Messrs.

Barnum and Bailey themselves could not have put on a better show. Mothers held up their children and pointed me out to them as a fiend that would gobble them up in their sleep if they were bad. Boys pelted me with stones and rotten fruit. Young men vied to count coup on me thru the bars, and when I caught one by the wrist, his companions beat a tattoo on me with sticks. Maidens laughed at my hairiness and poked fun at my privates, which were shrunken with fear and hence excessively diminutive for a man my size.

It is no pleasant thing to be the object of a population's contempt and hatred. My senses forgotten, I growled and roared, threw such fruit and stones as landed within my reach at boys and women alike, rattled the bars of my cage, struck back futilely when I could find a target, and at last, after some hours of torture, collapsed in tears wrought of frustration and exhaustion, which only elicited more laughter and gibes. Dazed and near catatonia, I lay curled in a ball on the floor of my cage with my hands over my ears and my eyes closed against the sight of my tormentors.

"Stand, heathen! Look at me, and listen!"

More an animal than a heathen, for a heathen is at least a man, I stood as directed and looked for the second time on the face of the Preeminent One.

"I have brought you a gift that will repay you for your insolence yesterday," said he, and gestured by raising two fingers.

Immediately the wall of red and blue feathers at his left parted and the most woeful, pitiable creature I have seen to this day was propelled out of the crowd and stumbled toward my cage, which he grasped with his hands in order to keep from falling down. He was naked as I, his hair long and matted with filth. His body was covered with terrible suppurating sores. One eye was closed with an infection, and half his teeth, I saw when he bestowed a wide but vacant smile on me, were missing.

"Have you heard of a man who looks like that?" the Preeminent One asked.

"You know I have," said I, roused by my indignation. "The Scapeweed Goat. And it is a poor sad thing you have made of a decent human being."

The creature's smile widened when he heard his name. His mouth opened and he tried to talk, but made only a grunting sound, for his mind was utterly broken.

"You are wrong," said the Preeminent One. "He is the happiest of men, and beloved of every Noble Savage. There is no more blissful way to end a life."

"A pity," said I in my sweetest voice, "that a bloated, fat old man cannot share in that bliss." The Preeminent One's face turned red, but before he could speak I turned my attention to the Scapeweed Goat and held my hand out to him. "It will be over soon, friend," said I, touching his hand tenderly. "Soon you will be free."

He did not like being touched. His smile turned into a snarl, and he shook the bars of my cage and hissed at me in his rage. And it was then, when he hissed like a cat, that I saw them and recoiled in horror. For on each side of his face, extending from the corners of his mouth up his cheeks, four furrowed white scars that imitated a cat's whiskers shone thru the filth. "No!" cried I, my heart breaking. "It cannot be!"

"Yes," said the Preeminent One in his smugness.

If he and his minions had sought to make my final hours as wretchedly miserable as possible, they had succeeded marvelously, and he knew it.

"David's son, Matthew, whose life we saved that he might give it to us as a sacrifice."

March 7

It is high noon. Andrew and I have just returned from the floor of the valley. The trail is treacherous but should be in excellent condition when I leave in the morning. I will write now and tonight in order to finish my story, which is just as well because I could not sleep in any case.

I saw a mountain falcon this morning. There is no food for him here yet for the floor is still covered by many feet of snow and the small prey the hunting birds eat are well hidden or have yet to return. The fact that he is here is a good omen tho, for birds, like other animals, are natural prognosticators of weather. He would not hover over my valley if he did not expect to find food. So he proves to me that the weather will hold, as if I needed more proof than the feeling in my bones. He was a fine sight, hanging there. Falcons are my favorite birds. If the Noble Savages were right about returning to life in the form of an animal, I should like to be a mountain falcon.

Andrew says he is perfectly happy being a mouse and would not be anything else on a bet, not even a glutton and especially not a man. I should like to ask the glutton what he would rather be, if anything.

This is a glorious day. The early snow, the devastation of my supplies, the gluttons who killed Harry, the loss of my horse, and of course the gangrene that took my hand were reverses that would have broken a lesser man. The world has tested me once again and once again I have laughed in its face and will continue on my way a victor.

Andrew points out that I sang a different tune when my hand was rotting off. That is true, but I learned from the experience. The next time I am in dire straits, I will remember that I have the power to prevail if I will keep a cool head. And so, on my last day here, I come to the events of my last day in the valley Home.

The Noble Savages left me alone that day to ponder David's failure and the horror of his son's election, and to pass the hours in contemplation of the night and the ceremony of the Gesture of Propitiation, whose culmination I would presumably not live to see. Having been moved out of sight around the side of the meeting hall, I could only guess from the little David had told me what rituals the Noble Savages were observing. The Civilizers might have enlightened me, but the Guards had separated us so we could neither see one another nor converse, tho what difference it made escaped me since I was going to die. I could see from my new vantage place a grand procession trooping toward the lake, but nothing else. They could not stop me from hearing, some time later, a beating of drums and a long, eerie confusion of chants and wails that rose to a feverish pitch and then stopped abruptly and was replaced by utter silence.

As happened here when I thought I was going to die, I was seized that afternoon with a frantic listlessness. I wanted to do something to help myself, but my cause appeared utterly hopeless. My thoughts ran in circles and loops, raced hither and yon, and I could do naught but sit motionless, devoid of energy, in one corner of my cage.

My mind and body were two separate beings. My legs were weak as reeds, my hands hung nerveless on my wrists, my head was too great a weight to hold upright. And yet my senses were alert. I noted every twig that moved in the light breeze and every person or bird or dog that passed within my vision. A veritable din assailed my ears. The rustle of leaves, a dog barking, human voices that I could not have heard at any other time. The splash of water, the clucking of a hen, a baby cooing, and a bird's wings beating. My nose had become more sensitive than a dog's, and the air held no secrets from me. Beef and pork roasted over open fires. Fresh bread was taken from an oven and set to cool. I could smell oxen and pigs and goats, and distinguish the odor of their urine from my own. Once I detected the sweet mustiness of a woman in her time, which left me racked with self pity. It was as if, facing death, I gulped in life with my senses, as if they could in some magical way ward off death, as if, being so filled with life, I could be neither overcome nor claimed by death, and it should have to seek some less fortunate victim.

How strange then that I was so insensitive to time. I saw the shadows creep across the ground, noted how the light ran up my legs and struck me in the face. And yet I could not believe it when I heard the dull thud of hooves and looked up to see a file of yoked oxen approaching thru the trees. Within moments my cage was lifted and placed on a wagon like the one I had seen at the farm, and I found myself at the beginning of a procession of carts that lumbered out of town and struck a wide dirt path to the east.

I once read an account of the carts called tumbrels in the time of the Revolution in France, and of how their wheels creaked and rumbled over the cobblestones. Many of the unfortunate souls on their way to the guillotine rode in a trance, capable of comprehending neither their journey nor its end. Some others wept, and some raged and shouted vile curses at the jeering crowds that lined the streets of Paris. In contrast, our gloomy parade wended its forlorn way past shuttered houses and yards empty even of stock, so we might have passed thru a depopulated land. And once again, to the tune of that unearthly creak and groan of wagons, reason abandoned me and I cursed at the Guards and their God, and called them and their ancestors vile names, and suggested they commit unnatural acts with their mothers and sisters. I might as well have excoriated the piles of dung the oxen left in their wake, for the Guards pretended not to hear, and my fellow prisoners averted their faces from me and rode in stoic silence.

Our destination was Discovery Promontory, or more correctly its base at the sheer rock wall that was said to reveal the
Face of God. As we neared, the road climbed a low, curving
hill that proved to be the rim of the amphitheater David had
described, in which the Scapeweed Goat and his Ewe were to
be sacrificed at the culmination of the Feast of the Gesture of
Propitiation.

The Quakers worship simply, as do the Amish and Mennonites and others of their kind. Any other religion I have
heard of has held on to its adherents in part thru pomp,
mystery, and spectacle. I had deduced as much about the worship of the Universal Infinitude thru David's descriptions of
the various festivals, and my conclusions were the more confirmed by the amphitheater, which was a gem set in the wilderness. The theaters of the Greeks were not more beautiful,
and the cathedrals of the Roman Catholics are not more awe
inspiring, for no work of man could match the sheer rock wall
that rose a full five hundred feet straight out of the valley and
reduced any mere human who stood at its base to insignificance.

The amphitheater, once no more than a natural depression,
had been sculpted, shaped, and improved to better suit the
Noble Savages' purposes. Two hundred feet across, it formed
a semicircle around the center of the base of the escarpment.
The rim, which was covered with a thick stand of grass that
had turned brown and dry from the weather, was flat on the
top, wide enough for a pair of oxen to pull a wagon around in
a circle, and sloped gently ten or twelve feet down on both
inside and outside. The interior sloped rapidly some fifty feet
in deeply cut terraces to a smooth flat floor that filled half the
diameter of the amphitheater. Entrance to and egress from the
terraces and the floor were by a wide ramp bordered by normal
sized stairs. At what expense of labor I couldn't imagine, the
interior had been irrigated and was lush and green. In the
center, against the rock wall, a low platform of cut stone jutted

into the otherwise empty arena. Torches fitted to the tops of poles rose at intervals along the front and sides of the stage and along each terrace.

The Guards and peasants wasted little time with us. Quickly they dragged our wagons to the north end of the rim, turned them around, and then unhooked the oxen and led them away.

I had been prepared for almost anything, but not to be left alone on a hill in the middle of nowhere. To the west, a sea of trees hid New Rousseau and the lake. To the east, the Face of God rose over me. To the north, the precipice sloped down to the gentler hills that bounded Home. To the south, I could see the entire amphitheater and the Civilizers' cages in a line along the rim.

"Well, where did they go?" asked I, as unnerved by the silence as I had been by the creaking and groaning. "Is that what they do? Just leave us here?"

"Patience, friend," said the woman in the cage nearest mine.

"Patience!" I bellowed, and glared at her. "A pox on your patience!"

"They will return soon enough, and with every Noble Savage who ever lived."

"Every one?" sneered I. "Including the dead Aspirants?"

"Did not David tell thee that the dead, too, return on this night?" she asked.

"No. I know only that they are dead, and that they died in vain."

The woman stared at me as if my blasphemy might rub off and pollute her. Her body pressing the bars of her cage in order to get as far away from me as possible, she conferred at length in whispers with the man next in line before addressing me again. "Answer me this, then, friend, for we would know. We are taught that the people of the civilized world do not know or live in the Truth and do not worship the Universal Infinitude. Is this so?

"Hah!" said I. "There is no Universal Infinitude."

The woman paled, and I thought she would swoon.

"There is no Universal Infinitude!" I repeated, shouting so each of them could hear me. "He is a sham! A figment of your imaginations!"

The woman and the other six quickly kissed their closed fists in the circles made by their thumbs and forefingers. "Thou art sunk and mired in ignorance, man, which is no fault of thy own, but rather the Creator's plan, for the time that the civilized world will know Him is not yet at hand. E'en so," said she, gesturing to the rock wall, "thou art blessed, for art singled out to see His face ere thy death."

I could see no face, and said as much. "And just as well, too," added I, "for I have no desire to gaze upon the face of a God who kills those who believe in Him."

"Thou art mistaken, friend. Men will kill us. Not our God, who loves us."

"Fagh! Loves you enough to let men kill you?"

"The Universal Infinitude hath given us life, and should any men strip that life from us, He will again enfold our souls in His immensity."

"Is it possible you truly believe such foolishness?" asked I, as astounded as I was enraged.

She was certain in her faith. "Is it possible that we should not, when our God hath given us all that is good and beautiful in life?"

"And evil and debased and foul and ugly as well?" I persisted.

"By the white stag and the black birds that eat of the 'scapeweed, and God's face in the rock, He promises us that we shall live forever!"

"Lies!" cried I. "All lies, every last word!"

The woman fixed me with a steely glare. "There is an Evil One, and thou art he, come among us." She needed no prompting from her fellows for her final retort. "We will have naught to do with thee, but turn our backs on thee and gladly die in the name of the Holy Infinitude, who is our life and our hope." And without another word she and the other Civilizers turned to the Face of God and raised their arms and eyes to Him, and filled the valley with their cries of love and faith.

I was tempted to tell them the history of the founding of their religion as David had related it to me, but my heart recoiled from the shame of so cruelly attacking their belief, and my anger abated. I had no more argument with the Civilizers than I had had with the farmer and his wife and children, for they were in contention with the authorities who had sent Guards to kill my wife and child. I had neither right nor reason to deride their hope and question their faith. What did it matter whether after their deaths they turned into lizards or lions or went to Heaven or Hell or merely ceased to exist? If their souls transmigrated, they would be happy. If they went to Heaven or Hell, they would no doubt be surprised but none the less existent. And if they merely ceased to exist, then the whole question would be meaningless. In any case, my spite would make the final hours of their lives miserable, which would be a mean and shameful act on my part. Killing Guards and Adepts was one thing, but bestowing pain and anguish on innocents was another, which I would have no part of.

More to the point, which struck me in the pit of my stomach, it dawned on me that I had but to change the name Universal Infinitude to Jesus and God, and the Civilizers would have spoken the very words I had been taught and had sworn by since the cradle. And every argument I had made against the Universal Infinitude I might have made against Christianity, the faith of my fathers, which had been my strength.

I did not have long to dwell on that unhappy and ironic state of affairs tho, for in the meantime the sun had dropped almost to the tops of the western hills. In the distance, underlying the prayers of the Civilizers, I thought I could hear the rumble of voices and the tramp of many feet. And whether it was so or not, the air seemed to grow thick and heavy, as before a storm.

Alone and huddled in one corner of my cage, I tried but was not able to pray to my Maker, for in my zeal to subvert the Noble Savages' faith, I had undermined my own.

March 8

How many times may a man be a complete ass and survive? To be caught and caged by a superior force is understandable. To walk into a cage and clap to the door and lock it and throw away the key by oneself unbidden is beyond reason, and the act of an utter fool.

I should have finished this account yesterday and been safely camped out halfway down the other side of the mountain at this very moment, but I am still here. In my anger, I first blamed the glutton. The truth is that the guilt is my own.

All was well when I finished writing yesterday. The sun was shining. Andrew and I strolled down to the beginning of the trail, which was as nearly open as I could wish. I spent an hour improving the first two straightaways and the first switchback in order to speed my departure today, and then we returned to the cabin where I ate some and dozed in the sun.

The cry of the mountain falcon, which is always welcome, woke me. I rose and stretched and, as has been my frequent pleasure these past few days, fetched my glass for a peek at the trail. And saw, halfway up it, the glutton!

I have not written much about my trail save for its presence and steepness. A trail is a trail, after all. But it is important to know that it ascends in switchbacks and in one spot, a third of the way up the mountain, lies but three hundred yards across an abyss from my porch. There was an older, steeper, and more dangerous trail one or two hundred yards farther south when I arrived in this valley, but I extended it and made a better switchback that had the added advantage of being close enough to be defended from my porch.

With my glass resting in the shooting fork on the roof post, I had the best look at the glutton ever. I believe the scoundrel must have sensed my eye on him, because he stopped and looked directly into my glass. He might have been no more than a dozen yards away from me. He did not look so malevolent by day. Rather, I would say, cunning and somewhat smug, with bright eyes and a small but toothy mouth that was opened in what I took to be a grin at my expense.

"What is he doing?" asked Andrew from his perch on my shoulder.

"Leaving," said I, snapping closed my glass and heading inside my cabin. "The son of a bitch is leaving. He thinks!"

I had forgone shooting him, even fed him, and there he was a quarter of the way up the trail I had cleaned but two hours earlier. I was weak and emaciated, and he was healthy and as sleek as a cat in a fishery from eating my meat, both what he had stolen and what I had given him. The damned ungrateful glutton had defeated me at every turn, and then thought to rub salt in my wounds, which I was not going to allow without some say in the matter.

He had doubled back on himself by the time I returned to the porch with my buffalo gun. Quickly I set Andrew down, laid my gun on the shooting fork, and drew a bead on the switchback. Directly, the glutton bounded up the trail, and I fired just as he paused to reverse his direction. The first shot missed but also startled him, for he leaped backward and almost fell off the mountain, which would have been funny had I had time to be amused. It is no easy task to reload with one hand. I propped the butt on my shoulder, steadied the gun with my forearm, opened the breech, reloaded with one of the cartridges I was carrying between my teeth, and was ready to fire a second shot just as he turned the corner. This one hit him at least a glancing blow, for he rolled over into the wall of the mountain. I had just reloaded by the time he recovered, and fired again, but the bullet was low.

I cannot imagine why fate decreed the calamity that followed. Directly after the bullet hit I heard the whine of a ricochet, and immediately a cracking sound as a rock that must have been loosened by ice broke free from the face of the mountain. Before I could say Jack Straw, the rock struck another and a whole chunk of the face crumbled and fell away in a small avalanche. On its edge, bouncing from ledge to ledge, the glutton was carried along by the rocks and fell into the valley, where he disappeared from sight.

I was too numbed to move. Andrew started jabbering. The falcon cried out, tipped on one wing, and slipped out of sight around a peak. At last, my heart in my throat, I put down my gun and took up my glass, and saw thru it a perfectly sloped pile of debris across both sections of the trail.

Cutting off my hand was hard to do, but easy in the sense that I had no choice in the matter if I wanted to live. Walking up my trail to the slide I had created was infinitely harder because the slide was the result of sheer stupidity, as Andrew was generous enough to point out. There was no sign of the glutton, so I suppose he was off licking his wounds.

The trail was in worse shape than I had feared. The mountain had caved in scant yards above the switchback, and the slide covered both sections so I could not tell their condition. At first I hoped I could climb the slide, but the rocks were so loose that to step on them was to start them rolling like marbles. Clearing them away being my only choice, I set to work, but had to stop before I finished because I did not want to be out after dark with a wounded glutton on the loose in the vicinity.

I went to bed last night after banking my hopes like a fire against the winter night, but fear they are utterly extinguished. I was back up the trail this morning at first light and had the lower section cleared by noon so I could inch my way along it, but only as far as the switchback. There I can stand as on a platform built into the side of the mountain. Beyond it I can walk ten feet, and beyond that there is nothing but the sheer face of the mountain for another thirty. My trail is not blocked but impassable none the less since I cannot walk on air, and I do not yet know what I will do to remedy the situation or how I will get out of here.

March 10

Damn me, but this is hard work for a one handed man who is short both on fingers and rations. I have not missed the little finger of my right hand for many years, but I should be glad to have it back on me now.

I am building a ladder to reach the twenty feet from the lower to the upper sections of the trail. I have cut and notched two long poles and lugged them up the trail. I wanted to build the whole thing at the bottom, but the weight of one pole alone under such treacherous conditions was the most I could handle. One, as it was, almost killed me when I lost it at the second switchback and it fell to the valley floor. I held on by the skin of a hen's tooth.

None the less, both are in place. Their bottoms are secured

in holes I chipped into the rock, and their tops extend two or three feet above the next section. They are tied together with the first rung, and the other rungs are lying there waiting for me tomorrow. That much work alone represents six trips up the trail, which is no mean task in itself.

Next I have to lash on the upper rungs. I have bound two forked sticks to my left forearm. The underneath one points toward my elbow so I can use it as a hook by which I can hold on to a rung or side pole. The upper one protrudes like a V so I can support a rung while I lash it in place with my good right hand. I am not so much worried about the lower rungs as I am the upper, for the ladder leans at a steep angle due to the narrowness of the trail, and my position will be the more precarious the higher I climb. The poles are springy and will bend in at the top when my weight is on them, which means I must devise some way to keep them off the face so I will have a firm footing while I lash on the upper rungs. I will be standing straight up before I finish, and perched over two hundred feet of empty air.

The stew I made three nights ago is gone. I am left with a pound or two of grain that is cooking with horse meat and bear fat as I write.

Andrew is alive and well, and has taken to foraging underneath the snow, as is not only natural but now necessary since I give him no more of my food. The glutton is well too, damn his soul to Hell. He prowls around my cabin by day when I am not here and has half destroyed the barricade over the door to Duke's shed, so I have moved as much of my horse meat as possible inside here since I have neither time nor energy for repairs. I threw him another rack of ribs tonight, not so much out of charity as in the hope that he will not try to break into my cabin tomorrow.

I am wearied almost beyond thought.

March 13

& I am conspired against and utterly confounded.

The first five rungs went up fast and easily. By the sixth the poles were bent in against the wall. I spent the rest of that day devising props to hold them out from the wall, and then working over my head to install them while standing ten feet above the ground on a bouncing, shaking ladder balanced over the abyss below me.

Yesterday was worse. The closer I got to the top the shakier was my platform, especially since a wind had come up. After climbing up and down all day, I was within one rung of my goal and could lay my arm on the upper trail when my legs failed me.

No matter. I would carry my gear with me in the morning, lash on the final rung, tie my meager pack to a rope, and climb out. From then on it would be a simple matter of hauling up my pack, shouldering it, and walking out. Trembling like an aspen, I staggered back here, where I fell into bed and asleep without any food.

But nothing is so simple. I woke in the middle of the night to a howling wind and went outside to find the air filled with snow. This morning I could see that my ladder had blown down, and now a full winter storm is raging.

I ate my last bowl of gruel for supper tonight, and am now without grain or berries or anything else save horse meat and bear fat and my one tin of peaches.

I am at my wit's end.

March 21

———————————————————————————

God damn the glutton and his dead mate, and God damn this never ending snow and ice. I do not deserve this fate after all I have gone thru in this life.

I am starving to death and have got the scurvy. A tooth fell out this morning. If I had killed Duke earlier when he had some fat left on him I would fare better. But then, if I had dug my cubbyhole bigger I would have elk meat. If I had protected my larder I would have grain. If if if. If I had left in August I never would have come to this pass, and if I were David I would be dead already. I would trade all the ifs in the world for a potato, and the potato for a way out of here.

I have drawn on every piece of paper I can find and stuck them up on my walls so I am not alone. My beautiful K greets me each way I turn. I have depicted my son as he appeared to me the night of my vision. Even David is here, and I sometimes imagine that we talk. Andrew thinks I have gone mad and keeps his distance when he visits me. That is a wise decision, because I would no more hesitate to eat a mouse than the glutton would hesitate to eat me.

I saw a play called Macbeth by Wm. Shakespeare in San Francisco once. In it three witches were gathered around a boiling cauldron into which they had thrown an eye of a newt and a tongue of a frog and other delectables. I liken my mind to that cauldron, into which have been thrown the memories of my life, and now one and now another rises up to the top where I view it momentarily before it sinks again into the seething mess.

None the less, I want to finish my tale of the Noble Savages and the Scapeweed Goat, and to help me I have drawn a picture of that night as I remember it. Sadly, I lack pigments, but never mind. Black ink will serve, and my mind's eye will supply the oranges and yellows of torch light and the bright hues of the Noble Savages' costumes.

My ears had not lied to me. No sooner had I turned than I could see figures emerge from the gloom under the trees. First came a phalanx of young men leaping and running wildly around a mass of red and blue that was the Conclave and the lesser Adepts. Behind them the town people and the peasants, who were surrounded by a loose ring of Guards in their drab paint, stretched in a disorderly mob down the avenue I had come along an hour earlier. I could see none of their faces, but they had dressed for the occasion in a multitude of bright colors and were a happy lot to judge by their shouts and laughter.

Suddenly a ram's horn sounded behind me. Turning, I saw high up on Discovery Promontory the minuscule figure of a man and heard again, six times, the single mellow note.

Immediately a vast and complete hush fell over the procession. The young men raced ahead and formed a double line up the slope of the hill. Between them the Preeminent One strode alone to the summit. Once there, he climbed onto what looked like a low platform that put him too in the light, and stood in silence for a moment before lifting his arms and calling out to the Face of God, "Behold! I am come to Thee with Thy people, and together we have brought Thee a sacrifice of a Scapeweed Goat and his Ewe, and pray that Thou findest them acceptable in Thy sight!"

I do not know where they hid the drums. In some secret cavern in the Face of God or under the rock platform perhaps, for the heavy throbbing at the tempo of a heart beating emanated from the center of the amphitheater and filled the air. At the same time, the young men in the double line produced torches that they lit in a manner unknown to me, and sped off to kindle the torches around the platform and along the terraces, and then ran back to the Preeminent One.

Mr. P. T. Barnum could not have done it better, for suddenly the Preeminent One began to glide across the top of the rim, dropped smoothly over the edge, and continued down the ramp on a wheeled platform that tilted to remain level. Bathed in torch light, he moved like a statue in an Easter parade, followed by the Conclave and the rest of the Adepts. Behind them the masses slowly spilled over the rim and spread to either side, filling the terraces.

Beside me the woman and the other Civilizers joined the throng below in watching the sunlight slide up the Face of God. And when it reached the very top, so only a golden pinnacle remained, the drums stopped and the horn blower stood sideways and raised his horn. In a second only the man was lit, and even as the light lifted off him, he lowered the horn to his lips and blew a single blast that was immediately answered by a thunderous resumption of the drums and an ear splitting roar from the assembled Noble Savages.

The most awe full sound I have heard since then was at the town of Gettysburg where, one July morning many years ago, the thunder of artillery rolled over the landscape like a juggernaut that would crush every living thing in its path. The roar of the drums and the crowd was as elemental, to be felt in the bones and guts and blood. The hairs on my neck raised on end as a steady, deep, indecipherable chant filled the amphitheater and echoed off the Face of God.

The Noble Savages were gripped in a religious frenzy. Arms raised and torsos swaying, they had become transmogrified into a mindless beast whose surface was in constant motion but that moved nowhere, like a den of snakes that has been disturbed, or a blanket of swarming bees that has lighted on a vine.

The Civilizers were as caught up as their executioners. Mesmerized, poor miserable naked creatures, they chanted and swayed in time with the rest. Below them, past the sea of humanity, the Preeminent One, his minions, and the Guards who lined the edge of the platform stood motionless.

They were not above using every trick in the book. The drums and chanting had gone on for some minutes when a great white cloud of smoke that totally obscured the Preeminent One erupted from a crevice in the floor of the platform. After it, cherry red and twinkling with yellow and blue and white, a column of fire spouted skyward. The din raised by the Noble Savages increased, if that were possible, until the Preeminent One was seen to rise into the air and, as if standing on a pillar of flames, tower over the assemblage. There, drinking in power from the wild drumbeats and fierce, insistent chants, he stood as majestic and awe inspiring as a malevolent, primordial idol found in a hidden jungle temple.

Such a display of ecstasy could not continue forever. Suddenly, looking like a great bird about to take flight, the Preeminent One raised his arms. Immediately the drumbeats and the chanting ceased, leaving only the last wave of echoes to wash across the enraptured tribe and diminish as it spread out over the valley.

"He is pleased with you!" the Preeminent One roared.

"We are nothing in His sight!" the Noble Savages responded.

"He is pleased with you!"

"We are His children and glory in His love!"

"He is pleased with you!"

"All glory to the Universal Infinitude, who reigns over all life forever and ever!"

"Then in His name, let the Feast of the Gesture of Propitiation begin!"

The flames rose to conceal the Preeminent One. As he disappeared, all heads turned to the center of the hill surrounding the amphitheater. There, one after another, a line of a dozen brightly painted men ran into the light and rolled like human cannon balls down the ramp into the arena. At the same time, a stream of fire in the shape of a semicircle ran out from the corners of the platform and met in the middle of the floor. Heels over head, twisting like pin wheels, the men leaped the fire and took their spots in the light, and then proceeded to give a demonstration of the art of tumbling that was slick enough to play to royalty.

Mundane tho many of the tricks were, they were artfully performed. The tumblers leaped, rolled, and walked on their hands. One stood upside down on his hand on another's head and spread his legs for his fellows to dive thru. Finally a drum began to beat and the Noble Savages commenced a cadenced applause. In response one man rolled to the center of the arena on a ball. No sooner had he arrived than two others leaped to his shoulders, where they balanced side by side by holding hands. Directly, three more were catapulted by their fellows on the ground to the shoulders of the top two, so they made an inverted pyramid. Just when they seemed to lose their balance and fall, the top three flipped in the air and landed on three balls that had been rolled out, the two in the middle flipped and landed on the shoulders of the three, and extended a hand to the lower man, who was thrown into the air and landed atop the middle two, so the pyramid was reversed, which trick the Noble Savages rewarded with thunderous applause.

The tumblers were only the first act. After them came jugglers who juggled every manner of thing from cabbages to pigs' heads to lit torches. One, the most adept of them, juggled at the same time a lit torch, a cabbage, a fish, a broad bladed knife, and a ram's horn. After him dancers took the stage, and then the Guards, who put on an exhibition of wrestling and unarmed combat. For their finale one man threw knives and another shot arrows at a third, who without being touched performed the Weaving Dance right to their feet, where he disarmed them both. The demonstration was impressive on its own, as well as being a veiled warning to any Noble Savage who might be tempted to wander or oppose a Guard.

Few would believe that a man could forget that he faces death in an hour or two. Yet death, being the last thing he admits can happen to him, is easily forgotten, tho never for long, for as much as his mind may wander, a queasy feeling in the pit of the stomach is sure to remind him that his hours are numbered. The fear rises and falls, boils to the surface and is suppressed, grips the vitals and relaxes its hold, and always returns with that hollow feeling of dismay when the heart lurches and panic threatens to overthrow him. Thus it was that the tumbling and dancing and mock combat were diversions that lasted not half long enough.

I was less distracted by the speeches that followed. The Chief Guard eulogized his predecessor and spoke of the added responsibilities of the Guards in those dangerous times. He promised that the Guards had accepted those responsibilities. He praised those who kept watch for the common good, and warned any who would undermine the welfare of Home that they would be apprehended and punished severely. He solicited the assistance of each true and devout Noble Savage in the unending war against the unrest and discord fomented by certain heretical factions and civic traitors from within their own number. He promised eternal vigilance against invaders from the outside. If any doubted the Guards' resolve in either of these matters, they had but to gaze upon the line of cages on the rim of the amphitheater. He did not enjoy taking life, but would take as many as were required, and give his own if necessary, that the children of the Universal Infinitude should remain pure and continue to deserve His blessings and enjoy His love.

I had no trouble remembering my role in the night's proceedings, and it wasn't so much the wind that had sprung up that raised the bumps on my arms as it was the menace in the four thousand pair of eyes directed at me.

The Chief Administrator was the next to speak. He rhapsodized about crops and livestock and how healthy and happy the Noble Savages were due to the salutary combination of their diligence in labor and their zeal in praising the Universal Infinitude. He said that the Universal Infinitude was the sun and the Noble Savages the moon, and that they shone only thru the magnanimity of the light thrown by Him. He went on and on in the manner of orators who have little to say but a great deal of time to say it in, and tho he undoubtedly made other salient points, I paid him little attention.

The Preeminent One spoke last. His speech promised to be short, for it was to culminate with the executions and the Gesture of Propitiation, which would be carried out and made under the watchful eye of the Universal Infinitude, whose face would appear when the moon bathed the wall. No moon ever rose faster, and no words of love and devotion and worship were ever more ominous. I scarce heard them, indeed, for no sooner had he begun to speak than the Guards began to wheel us down the slope into the arena.

The Civilizers were to die first and then, as the greater prize, I, followed by the Gesture of Propitiation by the poor Scapeweed Goat and his Ewe. One by one the tongues were taken off our wagons, and in their place were installed hooks that fastened to the same ropes that had let the Preeminent One's platform down the ramp. One by one, as the whole line of us inched along, the Civilizers' cages were hooked to the rope and made that maddeningly slow descent.

The Preeminent One, astounded and amazed that any Noble Savage could deny the Infinitude and betray his own kind, gazed sorrowfully on the Civilizers' cages as they were wheeled into position. Only two wagons were left on the rim, namely mine and one filled with supplies. The doors at the back of the supply wagon were open. Inside, a Guard had taken the lid off a wooden keg and had begun to measure an oily white liquid into individual flasks when the Scapeweed Goat and his Ewe were shepherded by three young Adepts into the light of the torches.

I do not know if the poor creatures had any idea of what their fate was to be. Their eyes were blank and they walked listlessly and obeyed the Adepts without question. The Adepts spoke to the Guard in the wagon, who handed one of them a pair of small vials.

"You want?" asked one of the Adepts of the Scapeweed Goat. "It will make thee feel good!"

The Scapeweed Goat grunted and trustingly held out his hand.

"Thy woman too," said the Adept, holding out the second vial to the Ewe. "Drink. It is for thee alone."

"Do not touch it!" cried I, knowing it was the aphrodisiac and hoping, for David's sake, that his son might be spared that ignominy, if nothing else. "No no no! It is bad for you. Bad for you!"

The Guard didn't need to be told his duty. Leaving the top off the keg, he leaped out of the wagon, pulled a torch from its hole in the ground, and ran to my cage. "Be quiet!" he shouted, waving the torch at me.

"Ha!" said I. "They are going to kill me, so I will say what I want. Do not drink it!" I shouted at the Scapeweed Goat and his Ewe. "Do not drink it! Do not drink it!"

Our argument had drawn attention, for if the voices of the speakers on the platform could be heard everywhere in the amphitheater, so could ours. The Preeminent One stopped in the middle of his remarks and looked up at us. Four thousand heads and pairs of eye turned to see what was happening. Embarrassed, the Adepts whispered furiously at the Guard to shut me up, and the Guard in response jabbed the torch at me thru the bars of the cage.

"Do not drink it!" cried I again, dodging the torch.

The Adept cupped the back of the Scapeweed Goat's head with one hand, put the vial to his lips with his other, and helped him drink.

"Damn you!" cried I as the Ewe accepted her portion. "God damn your heathen souls to Hell!"

They had never executed an Outsider before and so had no idea of what to expect from one. Certainly not, at least from me, the docility of the caged Civilizers. The Preeminent One raised his arms for silence from the muttering throng, but few were looking in his direction. Meanwhile, two or three dozen Civilizers in the crowd took advantage of the distraction and executed their plan then instead of some minutes later by leaping down from the terraces, pulling long knives from under their capes, and running forward to free their fellows.

The Guards stationed along the rim saw them first and raised a shout. Himself distracted, my Guard looked to see what the trouble was about, and in that lapse lost his life, for I grabbed his torch with one hand and his hair with the other, knocked him senseless by jerking his head against the bars of the cage, and choked him.

The Guards below could not see the Civilizers' advance because the wagons obstructed their view, and so thought the trouble was on the rim. The Adepts who had fed the Scapeweed Goat and his Ewe left those two alone and ran and slid down thru the grass to the uppermost row of terraces in order to calm the peasants, who had begun to mill about in their confined spaces.

The Civilizers' plan was well thought out, and they were fast. Before the Preeminent One or the Guards were aware of their bold move, they had hacked open the doors of the cages. The Guards above, who could well see what was happening on the floor of the arena, leaped down from terrace to terrace, further confusing the peasants.

The Scapeweed Goat and his Ewe might have thought this

show was put on for them. So delighted were they that they danced and leaped maniacally about in front of my cage.

"Run!" I shouted at them to no effect. "Run, Matthew!"

I do not know how long it had been since anyone had called him by his name. Hearing it tho, it was as if he partially recalled his former life, and his glee soured and he stood in one spot with his head swaying back and forth in the manner of a man who has been struck and knows not whence came the blow.

"Run, damn your hide! In your father David's name, run! He loved you, you idiot, and since he is dead, the least you can do is live!"

What goes thru a poor torn mind that has been so abused by substances best avoided by mankind? Did his father's name touch him in some secret recess of his addled brain? Did he remember the love they had shared in his youth? Perhaps I did Matthew a disfavor. Perhaps he would have been better off dying, no matter how ignominiously, in a fog induced by drugs. No doubt he was so far divorced from reality that he could never be put to rights. However warped and distorted his view tho, there was still some part deep inside him that was not totally corrupted, for of a sudden he seemed to be stricken with a severe agitation. Leaping now here and now there, he struck at chimeras and roared in anger. More like an ape than a human, he caught a Guard who would have restrained him and threw him bodily down the slope onto the terraces.

Having set him loose, I could not stop him. A mad man, he ripped the open doors of the supply wagon from their leather hinges and sent them spinning into the spectators, then climbed inside. A moment later vessels filled with the milky white liquid that produced the Smoke of Retribution flew thru the air, struck the ground, and broke open and spilled their contents in the grass. One side of the wagon ruptured. Thru it, a keg flew out and burst open. Then he climbed out and leaped onto the backs of the oxen, screaming at them and kicking them and driving them into a lurching run.

No one but I saw him, for the scene below had dissolved into utter chaos. The Civilizers had attacked the Guards, who were for the most part without weapons and soon outnumbered. Seeing them driven back, the spectators, who were drunk on 'scapeweed, jumped by the hundreds from terrace to arena and joined the fray. Men, women, and children fought the Civilizers, the Guards, and each other, and the Adepts, who sought to calm them, were severely handled.

I do not know why I threw the torch. I tell myself I wanted to add to the confusion, and perhaps that is true. The result, however, was catastrophic, for it landed in the long dry grass and set it afire. Fanned by the breeze, the fire spread quickly, and from it, where the grass was soaked by the liquid that produced the Smoke of Retribution, rose a dense white smoke that rolled down the hill in billows. Within seconds the fire reached the broken keg and set the oil to burning fiercely. Along it raced until it caught the wagon, which had broken apart at the top of the ramp. And before my eyes, the open keg caught fire and, like a bomb, rolled burning and smoking down the ramp into the midst of virtually all the Noble Savages in the world.

The wind and the weight of the smoke protected me. Driven toward the arena by the wind, falling of its own weight, the cloud filled the arena and covered everyone caught underneath it. What happened, how they died, I could not tell because I could not see them. I knew only that their cries became more and more feeble, and at last faded away to silence.

And this is the picture I have drawn, and that I look at as I pause from time to time to gather my thoughts. The drawing is accurate in its every detail.

This is the way the moon shone on the cloud of smoke that covered four thousand dead souls like a blanket.

You cannot hear their moans, but this is exactly how the Scapeweed Goat and his Ewe stood, front to back, as they swayed from side to side in their mindless copulation.

And this too, I swear it, is a precise depiction of the Face of God, which looked down in the moonlight on His chosen people.

March 28

A week has gone by and I am no better off now than when I last wrote. This will be my last entry, and it is all I can do to summon the energy to write.

The snow stopped two days ago, but has not begun to melt. The glutton prowls around my door every night. He has broken into Duke's shed and I assume has stolen or fouled the last of the meat left in there. Never mind. My gut will tolerate neither horse meat nor bear fat, which runs thru me without stopping for so much as a by your leave. I am a poor specimen with the starvation and the scurvy, all skin and bones. Soon enough the rest of me will be no better off than my left hand, but I am too weak to care and will be as glad to go as to stay.

Andrew has made a nest in my beard since I told him I would not eat him. We sing to each other. I have taught him some ribald songs of the Barbary Coast, and he sings to me about the joys of being a mouse. He is a droll little fellow and makes me laugh, for which I thank him.

And so I have at last recounted the story of the Noble Savages and the Scapeweed Goat, and feel the better for the telling of it. As for what happened to the Scapeweed Goat, to David's son, I do not know. I took the knife from the Guard I had choked and cut the vines that closed my cage, and left Matthew and his Ewe copulating on the rim of the amphitheater that had become a theater of death I dared not look at. Instead, I took one of the torches and made my way back to New Rousseau where I found my clothes and my weapons, took some food to carry with me, and struck off into the night, neither to look back nor to return to those parts.

As for the Noble Savages, their leaders and religion had led them down a blind path and failed them so completely that their society was doomed, but I am sorry I threw the torch and was the immediate agent of their destruction. I have ever been haunted by the dead I left behind me, whom I swear I did not mean to kill. They have been a heavy burden to carry thru life.

But not one to be carried much longer. When I finish this I will wrap the pages well, secrete the bundle in the hole under the loose stone in my hearth, and say goodbye to Andrew. Next I will put on my summer shirt and open my tin of peaches and sit out on my porch, where the glutton may find and eat me without the trouble of breaking in my door. And then I will eat my peaches and watch the sun set. Soon enough, with my stomach filled with the summer sweetness of peaches and my eyes with my friends the stars, I will succumb to the cold, and sleep.